By the same author:

# Belfast Girls

# Danger Danger

# Angel in Flight:
## an Angel Murphy thriller

# The Seanachie:
## Tales of Old Seamus

**Cover design: Raymond McCullough**

Brother and sister Jik and Nora are bored and angry. Why does their Dad spend so much time since their mother's death drinking and ignoring them?

Why must he come home at all hours and fall downstairs like a fool?

Nora goes to church and lights a candle. The cross-looking sailor saint she particularly likes seems to grow enormous and come to life. Nora is too frightened to stay.

Nora and Jik go down secretly to their father's boat, the *Lady Molly*, at Howth marina.

There they meet the Snapper, the same cross-looking saint in a sailor's cap, who takes them back in time on the yacht, *Lady Molly*, to meet Cuchulain, the legendary Irish warrior, and others.

Jik and Nora plan to use their travels to find some way of stopping their father from drinking – but it's fun, too!

Or is it? When they meet the Druid priest who follows them into modern times, teams up with school bully Marty Flanagan, and threatens them, things start getting out of hand.

Meanwhile, Nora is more than interested in Sean, the boy they keep bumping into in the past …

Thanks to my husband, Raymond, for cover design, proof-reading the manuscript, editing and general encouragement.

# Gerry McCullough

Published by

Precious Oil
PUBLICATIONS
www.preciousoil.com/publications

ISBN 13: 978-0 9525785 7 4
ISBN 10: 0 9525785 7 3

First published **2012**

10a Listooder Road, Crossgar,
Downpatrick, Northern Ireland  BT30 9JE

*For: David, Lily, Oliver, William, Charlie, Daniel, Cullan,
and Charlotte.*

# Prologue

The boat deck creaked precariously under their feet.

There was a loud, ominous crackling from the sails.

Nora looked round her. Was she imagining it, or had everything suddenly grown darker?

A whirl of angry clouds scudded across the sky, and a fierce cold wind pulled her long, black hair loose from its clasp and whipped it about her face. Nora put her hands up to push the hair out of her eyes.

'Jik!' she yelled.

'Wow!' said Jik.

Nora knew he had shouted, but she could hardly hear him. His voice was faint against the creaking of the ropes and the flapping of the sails as the mast swayed in the sudden gale.

She felt herself staggering as the *Lady Molly* began bucketing about in the wild lashing of the waves. Seizing the grab rail she collapsed onto the bench behind her, and heard her own voice crying out, 'Snapper! Help!'

Jik, flung across the cockpit by a quick lurch sideways from the boat, landed on her knee, panting breathlessly.

'Wow!' he said again.

Unbelievingly, Nora realised that he was enjoying this.

He was mad!

They were both mad!

What did The Snapper mean by bringing them into this? He should have warned them!

She heard a soft laugh near her ear, and realised it was The Snapper. He smiled briefly at her, showing bright white teeth against his tanned skin. His curly white hair and beard flew round his face in the fierce wind. He was clutching his captain's hat with one hand.

'Hold on tight!' he roared. 'Nearly there!'

Then, abruptly, the noise of the gale died away, the boat settled down, and Nora was able to breathe again.

Strangely, though, it was still dark, although it should be the middle of a July afternoon.

But Nora had no time to wonder about that.

A hand seized her roughly by the arm, pulled her to her feet. A voice spoke into her face.

'Ha! What have we here? Stowaways, by my oath! Speak! Who are you, and what do you want with me, aboard *White Lady*?'

*White Lady?*

But just before the storm, they had been safely on board their own boat, *Lady Molly!* What was happening? What were they to do? Was there any way out? Any way to get home?

Nora, trembling with horror, could say nothing.

# Chapter One

It had all started just yesterday.

A baking hot July afternoon in the middle of Dublin. School over for the summer. Jik and Nora climbing the apple tree in their back garden.

It wasn't a big garden, and it wasn't a big apple tree. It was in the Rathmines district of Dublin. The houses were high and the gardens were hidden away behind the houses.

The tree was small and twisted and produced only small, sour apples. But Jik and Nora liked to climb it.

'Where's the Da?' asked Nora presently. She straddled one of the middle branches of the tree, and nibbled at a green apple which, she was sure, would not make her sick. Every few minutes she pushed her long, black hair out of her eyes with the back of the hand which held the apple.

It was their own apple. Not many of the guys at St. Mary and Joseph's had apples of their own. Eating it made Nora feel special.

'In his pit,' said her brother Jik. 'Sleeping it off, I suppose.'

Jik, his freckled face frowning in determination, had hoisted himself further up than Nora, so that he could see into the neighbouring garden. He stood on one of the higher branches, holding tightly, with one arm wrapped round the nearest part of the trunk. His other hand shielded his eyes from sun glare, as he peered over the high wall.

There was very little to see except the next door cat, fat and ginger, curled up beside the next door bin.

Jik was Captain Jack Sparrow, commander of a pirate ship, looking out for enemy vessels across a wide, blue range of sea. He didn't want to be reminded of his father, or made to think about him.

There was a pause.

'Maybe I should make him a cup of tea?' Nora suggested.

'Whatever,' said Jik.

His pleasant sun reddened face was crunched up in a scowl. He ran one hand through his bright red hair, lifting it back up from his forehead and eyes. A moment later it had fallen down again.

'What's the use?' he said. 'He'll get up in his own good time. Too late to take us to the Marina, I bet. It must be months since the last time he took us out on *Lady Molly.'*

'Was he down the pub last night, then?'

'Have a guess.'

'He was down the pub.'

'Right.'

'With Patsy Mulligan and Frankie Rafferty and that Bridie Gallagher, right?'

'Right.'

Nora said nothing for a few minutes. Then she burst out.

'Why does he do it, Jik? Ever since mammy died, he's been down the pub nearly every night. Why can't he stay home with us?'

Jik, at thirteen and a half, was a year older than Nora. He reckoned to know more about stuff than she did. And after all, she was only a girl. She couldn't be expected to understand about men.

'He misses Ma,' he said. Jik wouldn't say, 'Mammy', like Nora. Only kids did that. 'He needs company to help him forget.'

'Oh.'

'I suppose we should try to help him.'

'Oh.' Nora thought about it. 'Maybe I should make him that cup of tea, then.'

'Whatever,' said Jik again. He shrugged.

'But even if he does miss Ma, he doesn't need to go out boozing every night!' he burst out. 'He's just a loser, that's what. It's been over two years now. Time he got a grip on his drawers!'

'Jik!'

'Well, it is! What about us? He doesn't give a curse about us, and after all, he's the grown up and we're still kids! He ought to care!'

Nora was silent, watching Jik solemnly.

He had never been so open before.

Especially he had never referred to himself as a kid. Jik liked to think of himself as nearly grown up.

After a moment or two, Nora made up her mind. She slid carefully down the tree trunk.

# Chapter 2

She went into the kitchen and put the electric kettle on. She stuck two slices of bread in the toaster, checked that it was switched on at the wall, took butter and milk from the fridge, and sugar and tea bags from the jars on the shelf beside the kettle.

She reached on tiptoe to unhook the Da's special mug from high on the wall. It said 'Sailor Bill' on it in big red letters. It had a picture of a Captain Birdseye type, with white hair and curly beard and whiskers. It was a present from the Da's mates on the fishing boat he used to work on, before Granda died and left him a lot of money and the house in Rathmines.

Nora was very careful with the mug. If she broke it she knew her father would be very upset as well as very cross. The mug was special to him. It reminded him that once he had been a sailor.

When the kettle boiled, she made tea and then buttered the toast when it had popped up. She made sure to spread the butter right to the edges, the way the Da liked it. She carried the mug and toast upstairs on a tray, and knocked on his door.

There was a grunt from inside.

'It's me, Daddy,' Nora said. 'I've brought you some tea.'

The Da grunted again, and Nora pushed open the door and went in.

He was lying with his face half buried in the pillow, the duvet over most of him, but with one foot stretched out at the side. His bright red hair, as red as Jik's but much longer, stuck out in tufts from under the pillow.

As Nora came in, one vivid blue eye opened hazily and then closed again.

'Ta,' he managed. 'Just put it down on the table. Right.'

'You'd better wake up and get it before it's cold, Daddy.'

Colm Lavery groaned.

'Are you going to wake up and take us to the boat, Daddy?'

Another groan.

'Nora, pet – just leave me be, there's a good girl.'

Nora gave up.

Putting the tray down with a bit of a thud, she went out of the room. She didn't exactly bang the door behind her, but it was a near thing, and she certainly didn't close it quietly.

'It's not fair,' she thought. 'Why does he keep boozing and letting us down?'

Jik was still up the apple tree. Nora's face told him how useless her efforts had been.

5

'This is just pants!' Jik said. He scowled, and then shrugged.

'Why don't we just go on down to the sea ourselves?' he suggested.

'Well – I suppose we could – but we couldn't take the boat out.'

'I don't see why not,' Jik said argumentatively. 'I'm nearly fourteen, you know, and the Da taught me how to manage *Lady Molly* years ago. When he bought her. And you aren't too bad with ropes and things,' he added graciously.

Nora, while appreciating the compliment, was still doubtful. 'You won't be fourteen for more than another six months,' she reminded him. 'And the Da made us promise never to touch the boat when he wasn't there.'

'I don't see that that counts any more. He's never there these days. When he got us to promise, he took us out in the boat at least once a week in decent weather, and a lot more in the summer.'

Jik looked hopefully at his sister. However, one glance was enough to tell him that Nora was wearing her stubborn look, her teeth catching her under lip and her chin jutting firmly out.

'Oh, all right,' he said. 'But how long do you mean to let all this go on, then?'

'Perhaps he'll stay in tonight. I know!' exclaimed Nora hopefully. 'We could get him to tell us some stories. About when the *Mary Sue* got caught in the storm, when the Da was still working on her as a fisherman. And about our great, great – or whatever – granda, Peter Lavery, who invented radar hundreds of years ago!'

'It wasn't radar, dafthead. That was only invented some time round World War Two.' But Jik looked interested.

'Well, it was some very important invention to help steer ships, and he was cheated out of his rights in it. It's a very interesting story, and you know the Da loves telling us about it. We could get him to stay in. Then maybe he'd go to bed early, and be able to get up and take us to the sea tomorrow.'

They both felt excited at the idea of doing something about the situation.

'Well, okay. We'll try it,' Jik ruled. 'But if it doesn't work, then we can't just go on waiting for him day after day. Do you agree that if there's no change tomorrow, we'll take a bus and go down to the boat ourselves?'

Nora agreed. 'But I'm sure it will work,' she comforted herself silently. 'And I didn't promise to take the boat out – just to go down and see it.'

# Chapter Two

It was teatime before Colm surfaced.

He staggered to the bathroom, and they heard the loud flush of the toilet, followed by the sound of the shower.

Presently they heard him coming down the stairs. He was coming slowly, with a lot of pauses, and an occasional tripping noise followed by words they got scalped for using.

So nothing different, then.

The back door shot open and Colm tripped over the bin. Then he righted himself. 'Well, lads,' he said, in his jovial, sea captain's voice. 'Having fun, then?'

'No,' said Jik coldly.

Nora kicked him lightly, scrambled down the tree and ran over to the house.

Jik followed.

'Hey, time we ate, yes?' said Colm, attempting to maintain the cheery voice. 'How's about I order a pizza, okay?'

'That would be great, Daddy,' beamed Nora.

'No anchovies, mind,' stipulated Jik suspiciously. The Da's fondness for seafood was notorious.

'No anchovies it is, then, Jacob me old maty,' Colm agreed.

Anything, they could see, to keep on good terms with them. The guilt crept out of his eyes as they watched him trying to smile.

'And then perhaps we might play *Cluedo*, and you could tell us some of your stories,' suggested Nora innocently. 'You know we have that *Simpsons Cluedo* Auntie Mary bought us for Christmas, and we haven't played it with you since that one time. That would be great fun, Daddy. Please do!'

'Why not?' Colm agreed lightheartedly. 'Now, if it's not to be anchovies on this pizza, what alternative are you wanting?'

'Flame grilled chicken,' said Jik promptly.

'Pepperoni,' Nora added.

'Mushrooms.'

'Red peppers.'

'Tomatoes.'

'Sweetcorn and carmelised onions.'

'And three sorts of cheese.'

'And olives.'

Pause for breath.

'And red onions.'

'And green peppers.'

'Whoa, whoa!' said Colm, laughing. 'They won't be able to get more than that on board! A giant size pizza, it had better be then. And garlic bread and coleslaw?'

'Yep!' said Jik and Nora together.

Like, wow! This was something!

Colm went to the phone, and Nora dragged out the *Simpsons Cluedo* game from the corner cupboard.

Half an hour later, they were engrossed in the game. Colm was doing his Marge Simpson impression, to shouts of laughter from all three of them, and Nora was just about to denounce Bart Simpson with the necklace in the studio, when a ring at the doorbell announced the arrival of the pizza.

It was a lovely meal. Everyone had more than enough, and the leftovers were bundled up and put in the fridge, with a view to reheating them in the microwave at supper time if anyone was ever hungry again.

Then Nora asked the Da to tell them the story about great, great – whatever number of greats – Granda Lavery who had invented radar or something hundreds of years ago, or whenever, before anyone else had thought of it, and who had been swindled out of his rights, and who would have been a millionaire and have left an enormous fortune to his descendants if he had had his just deserts.

Colm was only too happy to tell the story.

'Ah, that was a man to be proud of,' he began, holding his last piece of pizza in one hand and a piece of kitchen roll to catch the drips in the other. 'Mind you, the family has done all right for itself ever since. It's not the loss of the money that matters so much. It's more the status, you see. Do you follow me? A man would have something to be proud of, if he could say, 'My great-great-granda invented radar before it was ever thought of.' But the secret was stolen from him back in the mists of time when he first came up with it.

# Chapter 2

'He was the sailing captain on the *Nancy Belle* when all this happened, and a very clever man, well educated in science and so on. A friend of Faraday, I'm told. He had given a deal of thought to the mysteries of steering the ship, and one night when he couldn't sleep, he got out of his bunk and dressed in the bare necessities of clothes and went for a stroll round the deck, while he thought about the needs of the helmsman, and how in foggy or murky weather he couldn't see the stars by night or the sun by day and couldn't see icebergs looming up or whatever, and how that made it so hard for him to steer the ship.

'And then he thought about the new invention of electric light, and the whole thing of electricity, and light waves, and other sorts of waves, and he looked up at the stars, and he thought, 'If you can be replaced by waves of electricity to give light, why not by some sort of waves to help with the steering?'

'And it was then that the first glimmering of his great idea came to him. He walked round the deck, and round the deck, and he thought.

'So it was then that it came to him that there was a way, if only he could be clear about it, where he could find out a method of steering, not by the stars or the compass, but by the new science. Waves that would tell him if any other ships or obstructions were in the way, even in the fog or the dark –'

The phone rang. Ding a ding a ding.

And went on ringing.

# Chapter Three

At first Colm himself was annoyed at the interruption.

It had been fun, playing with the kids, and telling them about their history as Laverys.

There was a lot to be proud of in the family history, and he wanted his son to be proud of it – and of course, his daughter, too, he added hastily to himself, remembering how his wife, Molly, used to tease him about his Irish upbringing as a male chauvinist pig.

'I'd better answer it, lads,' he said. 'But don't worry, I'll tell whoever it is that I'm booked up tonight. We have to finish that game of *Cluedo*, now. I'm just about to win, see?'

He grinned, and strode off to the phone in the hall.

Jik and Nora could hear him clearly.

'Hullo – hullo – oh, Bridie …'

'Well, I'm kinda busy, see …'

'Yes, I know I said …'

'So what's the plan …?'

'No, well, I've sorta told the kids …'

'Yeah, I know any time would be the same …'

'Ah, now, Bridie, I don't mean to let you down …'

'So, is Patsy coming too? ...'

'Ah, I know, it would be great crack …'

'Of course I want to see you …'

'Of course I care, babe …'

His voice sank lower.

Jik and Nora looked at each other.

'Maybe he won't,' Nora whispered. 'He's been enjoying it. He said he'd stay in …'

Her voice trailed off miserably, as Jik made his, 'Yeah, yeah,' face.

They sat, eyes down, trying to hear Colm's end of the conversation.

Then the door into the hall swung shut, and all sound from the phone was cut off.

It was ten minutes later before he came back in.

'Sorry, kids,' he said briefly. 'I forgot I'd promised a friend I'd go out tonight. It's really important. We can finish the game, and then you can watch the box until ten o'clock. Jik, I'm trusting you to see that you both get off to bed after that, right?' Jik muttered something inaudible, but Colm accepted it as agreement.

It didn't take long to finish the game. Nora won, but couldn't have cared.

At twelve forty, when the late film was over, they trailed miserably up to bed.

There was no sign of Colm yet. Jik reckoned it would be at least another hour before they heard him come in, or maybe more.

Nora wasn't sleepy.

She sat down at her desk, and fished out her diary from the inside pocket of her jacket where it hung on the back of her bedroom door.

She thought for a while about what she should say. Presently she got up and went over to the mirror above the dressing table.

Screwing up her eyes, Nora peered at her face.

Blue eyes, black hair.

A sort of Snow White image, but not so baby, she hoped.

And a white skin, of course.

She could remember her mother. It wasn't all that long ago.

She knew she looked a bit like her mother, because people always told her so. That was a good thing, wasn't it?

Nora went over to the wardrobe and brought out the photograph album. There were lots of photos of mammy.

Maybe Nora did look a bit like her.

That would be nice.

It would be great to look really beautiful, to have guys falling in love with her at first sight.

No one had so far, at least no one had said so.

It would be brill if Sean O'Reilly fell in love with her. He was too cool to say so, mind you. He'd probably just say he fancied her, or that she was a real honey, or something.

Maybe he would say that she was hot?

Nora sighed.

Some hope!

## Chapter 3

She went back to her desk and opened her diary.

*July 16. It's been another yuk day. The Da's a real pain. He mitched off over four hours ago to go boozing. Last orders musta been ages ago, so what's he doing now? Snogging that Bridie Gallagher, I bet.*

*I wish I could think of some way to make him stop all this. He was dead on, before mammy died.*

*Da was telling us about our great, etc. granda Peter Lavery again tonight. He seems to think a lot of him.*

*Maybe if great Granda Peter had got his rights, and the Da had that to be proud of, it might make him think more of himself, and maybe then he'd stop the boozing?*

*Tomorrow I've promised Jik to go down to the sea with him.*

*I'm a bit scared, right?*

*But I didn't promise to help take Lady Molly out, and I don't think he'll go by himself.*

*It's ages since we've seen the boat, and after all, when the Da bought her he said it was mainly so us kids could grow up knowing about boats, the way he did. We thought it would be a real gas.*

*But it's been a waste of dough instead, with us never getting out on her.*

*What's the use of having a boat if you never get to sail in her?*

*Maybe tomorrow morning I'll slip down to church and light a candle about all this mess.*

*Something needs to change soon, or I'll just run away, so I will!*

*45 days till I see Sean O'Reilly again. Don't want to be back at school except for seeing him. I hope he hasn't cut his hair over the summer. He's such a babe with it curling down over his eyes. Gonna stop writing this diary now and think about Sean instead, till I get to sleep.*

*Wonder if he'll speak to me next term?*

*Or maybe even ask me out?*

*Later.*

*Da came in at three o'clock or so. He was banging about downstairs, and then he came upstairs letting out a lot of moaning and carry-on. I was just nicely over to sleep, and he woke me right up.*

*I was near to shouting out to him to keep the clatter down, but I didn't.*

*Then Jik called out, 'Would you ever keep the noise down?' and he mumbled something about being sorry and went into his room.*

*Then he came out onto the landing and there was a thud and a bang and a sliding noise. Jik and me rushed out to see what was going on, and there was the Da at the foot of the stairs, one leg up and one down, not seeming to know where he was or what happened.*

*'Wha' – wha' …?' he muttered, and tried to stand up, and collapsed in a heap again.*

*Jik said, 'Eddie the Eagle strikes again, in his amazing skiing down the banisters trick.'*

*Jik was really angry.*

*Jik and me got the Da under the arms and dragged him to his feet, and then we made it up the stairs and dumped him in his room on the bed.*

*Jik was all for leaving him like that, but I got him to help take the Da's shoes off, and I got the duvet pulled over him with a bit of a tug.*

*Tried to go back to sleep again by thinking some more about Sean O'Reilly, but it didn't seem to work, so I got up and said my prayers again and wrote some more diary.*

*Feel very sleepy suddenly, so no more now.*

# Chapter Four

Next day Nora got up earlier than usual. With no one calling them for breakfast, and Colm sleeping later every day, it was a while since she'd bothered. It would be different when school started back, of course.

Nora had always loved going to the church with mammy. There was something very warm and cosy about it. Today she was going on her own, but that was all right. She'd got sort of used to it over the last two years. Jik never wanted to come, and the Da had stopped making the effort over the last ten months or so.

She slipped quietly into the back pew and knelt down.

She looked around her. The church was empty except for Father Ryan up at the altar.

Nora gazed at her favourite statue. It was only a head and shoulders, really. A man, with a beard, and a rather scowly, cross looking face, wearing what looked a bit like a sea captain's hat. A bit like the picture on the Da's mug, if he hadn't looked so angry. He had been there for so long, Father Ryan said, that no one remembered who he was, or even his name.

Nora liked him because Mammy and the Da used to make jokes about him, and the Da had called him, 'St. Stormy Weather, the sailors' saint.' She smiled as she remembered. Then, because it was something the Da had always done, she winked at him.

The happy memories suddenly became tears.

'Dear God,' prayed Nora, 'Can you please do something about the Da? Things are just awful these days.' She paused to reflect. Maybe He would like her to say some proper prayers as well as her own made up ones.

She spent some time repeating as much as she could remember of the more formal prayers of the church.

Then she rose to her feet and went over to the candles. She had some pocket money left. The Da was generous with pocket money whenever he thought about it, or when they reminded him.

Nora chose a lovely fat candle, paid for it, and set it up ready to light.

'Dear God,' she prayed, 'do you think you could help me and Jik to find great, great, great Granda's invention, and the proof that he really did invent it? Because maybe if the Da had something like that to be proud of, he'd catch himself on?'

Then she lit the candle, and watched, mesmerised, as the flame flickered higher, and the wax began to melt lower and lower.

Out of the dim shadowy darkness behind her, suddenly a voice spoke.

'Come on, Nora, what's all the crying about?'

Nora jumped several feet.

It must be Father Ryan.

But, no.

Father Ryan was still pottering about over at the far end of the church.

She turned her head, looked round cautiously.

Was it the light of the candle still dazzling her eyes?

Just beside her, on the shelf where the old sailor saint was perched, a glare like a floodlight shone its intense brilliance into the darkness all around.

For a moment, Nora was blinded.

She stared in bewilderment, and in growing panic, at the light.

'Don't be frightened, Nora,' said the same voice.

Peering through the brightness, Nora found that she could manage to see, though indistinctly.

But what was this she was seeing?

Had the old saint really turned his head to look directly at her?

She gazed at him in horror.

As she gazed, she could have sworn the saint winked at her!

Nora stood stock still for a moment.

Her legs felt paralysed. Would she ever be able to move them again?

The huge shadowy figure of the saint, so small a moment ago, loomed over her, enormous in the gloom, and growing even larger as she stood there looking. It seemed to be coming towards her.

Gathering the remnants of her courage round her like a comfort blanket, Nora bolted down the aisle, thrust open the doors to the outside world, and fled, trembling in every limb, back through the sunlit streets full of ordinary people, to the safe world of her own kitchen.

Jik was standing at the kitchen table, moodily buttering toast.

'Hi,' he greeted her. 'Don't ask, he isn't up yet. Where's the peanut butter?'

'Where you left it last time,' snapped Nora. 'You're the only one uses it.'

'Oh.'

The peanut butter was sitting on top of the fridge. Nora carefully didn't look.

She was not, N. O. T. not, going to run after Jik in a typically Irish girlie way, and fetch and carry for him.

Jik stood up and wandered aimlessly around, peering behind plates and opening cupboard doors.

After a few minutes, Nora couldn't stand it any more.

'If you'd use your eyes, it's on the fridge!' she shouted.

'Ta,' said Jik, unperturbed.

'Well,' he said, when he had transferred half the contents of the jar to his toast. 'So.'

Nora didn't look at him.

'So?' she muttered.

'So, how soon should we start?'

'We'd need to give him a chance, so,' argued Nora. 'If he's not up by two, we'll leave him a note and go on.'

'That's leaving it dead late!' objected Jik. 'We don't want to get there when the day's near over.'

'Take it or leave it. It's not fair to go off without giving him a chance.'

Jik said no more. Two o'clock would come soon enough.

And then for the Marina, and *Lady Molly*.

# Chapter Five

The best way was to catch the DART (the Dublin light railway) to Howth, where the Marina was.

That meant getting a bus into the City Centre first. They were lucky, there was a train just due to leave when they dived panting into the station just off Pearse Street.

Jik grabbed the window seat.

Nora was annoyed, but said nothing. She was still feeling upset.

Was she going mad, or what? Or did she just have a specially vivid imagination?

Her English teacher had said once that Nora had a great imagination – it was supposed to be a good thing. Nora found that she didn't much like it, all the same.

It was after three when they reached Howth, where Colm's boat, *Lady Molly*, was berthed.

'Can you remember the password into the Marina?' Nora asked with a worried frown.

'It'll have changed since we were last here,' Jik pointed out, 'but they know us, they'll let us in.'

They charged along the sea front, through the public gardens. The Marina was at the other end of Howth from the DART station.

The smell of the fish market went with them, and something about the way the sun was gleaming on the sea made them feel better about things.

It was a perfect day for the boat. There was a warm breeze, but the waves weren't too rough.

As they came nearer they could see the little rows of dancing boats along the pontoons, smiling in the sunlight, white and bright and sparkling.

'There's *Lady Molly!*' said Jik suddenly. 'See?'

Nora looked, squinted, and then saw.

*Lady Molly* gleamed fresh in the light. She rode proudly in the soft breeze, mast standing high, mainsail folded down along the boom and stowed in its bag; her other sail, the jib, rolled safely around the forestay. Her white and blue paint looked as shiny and spotless as the day Jik and Colm had put the final touches to her.

They caught their breath.

'Isn't she beautiful?' sighed Nora.

'Yeah.'

They could see the name along her side now. *Lady Molly – Molly* after their mother, and *Lady*, Colm had said, because both she and his wife were ladies in every line.

Nora thought wistfully that it was good that Mammy had been out in her a few times before the cancer took hold. At least she'd had that.

The desire to be out on the sparkling waves was growing on Nora. She told herself sternly that a promise was a promise. But it seemed hard to let the golden summer days go by without a single trip. Maybe Jik was right when he said the promise had been made under different circumstances, and didn't count now?

They went round to the side gate. A man and his wife were going through. No reason why they couldn't slip in at the same time.

Jik and Nora followed on the heels of the couple, and went carefully down the ramp.

They knew their way to the boat. Along the main pontoon. Turn right, then turn left.

There she was.

Moving carefully as they had been taught, first Jik and then Nora took one step on to the edge of the starboard side deck, brought up the second foot next to the first, while reaching for the grab rail on the cabin roof, swung one leg over the safety rail, then swung the other. Holding on to the grab rails, they moved along the side deck until they reached the cockpit, then stepped down onto the cockpit floor – the sole.

*Lady Molly* was a 21 footer. Big enough to have fun in, but not too big to be handled by two people, or even one who knew what he or she was doing.

Jik and Nora, safely aboard, looked around them with delight, remembering everything they saw, and reminding themselves about her.

There was the helm – the steering wheel – and beside it the cabin door, shut at the moment. Behind it, the two bunks and the galley made the boat into a real holiday delight. There was a sink with actual running water from the water tank in the bow, Nora remembered, and a gas cooking stove for meals.

She remembered the Da frying fish for the whole family on that stove, while Jik looked after the steering. Nothing had ever tasted better.

In the bow was another, much smaller cabin, with a further bunk, which held two at a pinch. Suddenly Nora let out a gasp.

'Jik!' she exclaimed. 'You won't be able to take her out even if it was right! You forgot the cabin's locked, and you'll need the other key for the engine as well, to start it!'

'Ah ha!' said Jik triumphantly. His freckled face broke into a wide grin. His red hair seemed to catch extra reflections from the sun.

He plunged one hand into the pocket of his jeans, and came out with a familiar bunch of keys.

'That's where you're wrong, my bold Nora! I remembered that we'd need the keys, and I nicked them from the Da's desk drawer this morning while you were out, and the old eedjit was snoring his head off.'

'Jik! Don't talk about him like that.'

'Well,' said Jik, 'maybe it's not too good. But if he would act a bit more sensibly I wouldn't do it.' He scowled again.

Then, recovering, he waved the keys in the air.

'So, nothing to stop us. Off and away! Okay?'

They stood looking at each other. Nora was never sure, afterwards, what she would have said. But at that crucial moment a loud voice assailed their ears.

'Jik! Nora!'

They turned guiltily. A man was hurrying towards them along the pontoon.

He looked vaguely familiar, and at first they both thought it must be one of Colm's sea-going friends, although he certainly seemed a lot older than Colm.

# Chapter Six

He was clearly a sailor, and looked like a captain, from his peaked cap down to his boots. White curly hair stuck out from beneath the cap and a white curly beard and whiskers covered half his face. His skin was red and weather beaten, his nose was long and sharp, and his eyes, which were bright blue, twinkled at them.

'So, lads, what's all this, then?' he began. 'Did your Dad give you permission to go aboard the *Lady Molly* by yourselves, the bold rascals that you are? I'll be bound he did no such thing!'

He had reached the boat by now, and he stood beaming up at them. Jik was the first to recover his voice.

'He wouldn't mind us just coming on board to see how she is ...' he began.

'Ah, but you'd be a liar if you told me that was all you were going to do, eh?' said the old captain. 'I know you better than that.'

'You know us?' It was Nora who expressed the surprise they both felt. A strange feeling was creeping over her.

'Known you all your lives!' laughed the captain. 'Do you tell me you don't know who I am?' He shook his head, in a pretence of sorrow. 'Well, well! I'm not so surprised at you, Jik, for it's a year or two since you've seen me, but you, Nora! Why only this morning you were winking at me! You left in a bit of a hurry, didn't you?'

Nora's mouth fell open.

'But, there,' went on the strange sailor, 'Let's not hold any grudges. Now, I know your Da would never allow you out in *Lady Molly* by yourselves, but sure I'm an old friend of his, and I'd be willing enough to take you out for a short trip, if you like. What do you say?'

'Who are you?' Nora burst out. She was half angry, half frightened. But there was nothing to be frightened about, surely, here in broad daylight in the middle of Howth Marina, with the place hiving with folks?

'If you think we should know you,' added Jik slowly, 'why don't you give us a name? I'm sorry if we seem rude, but you must see that we can't let someone take the Da's boat out, even to take us for a trip, unless we know who you are.'

The old man looked keenly at them. His blue eyes crinkled up, and his face took on an angry scowl.

'Are you sure you don't know?' he asked.

Jik felt a strange familiarity stealing over him. He still didn't really know who this was. But shouldn't he know?

And Nora, standing beside Jik and saying nothing – all at once Nora knew. But what was she going to say? Was she going to admit what she had seen? Was she going to make Jik think she was mad?

It would be so much easier to keep quiet!

But suddenly she found herself speaking.

'I know who you are!' she said. 'You're St. Stormy Weather, the sailors' saint – aren't you?'

Then she blushed furiously, because as she heard her own words they suddenly seemed ridiculous.

But Jik was speaking, too. 'I'm not sure who you are,' he said, 'but you're certainly someone I know. And you do look like that old saint, so!'

'Aha! Come to your senses, have you? I knew you were bound to recognise me sooner or later!'

The scowl disappeared. The old sailor began to twinkle at Jik and Nora again. Nora felt her fear slowly beginning to disappear.

'But you've got the name wrong,' he added. 'That's just your Da's nickname for me. Mind you, I don't rightly know what my real name ever was. For as long as I can remember, I've gone by yet another nickname. Allow me to introduce myself, lads. I'm The Snapper. Leastways, that's what my old mates used to call me in my sailing days. I never really knew why, for sure it's not in my nature to snap at anyone, unless they were making a queer fool of themselves! Anyway, Snapper it is, and has been for as long as I can remember, so you may call me that if it makes you feel easier to put a name to me.' He swept off his peaked cap and bowed extravagantly to them.

'But – I don't understand,' Jik stuttered. Suddenly it seemed impossible not to believe that The Snapper was who he claimed to be. But nevertheless –

# Chapter 6

'What are you doing here?' Jik asked. 'How did you get here, and why have you come?'

'Whoa, whoa, with the interrogation!' laughed The Snapper. He ticked the questions off on his fingers, giving an answer methodically to each in turn. 'Why? Oh, that's the easy one! I'm here at the request of the young lady. How – that's not for you to know, or for me either, for that matter. I was sent, is all I'm allowed to say. What for? Why, to help you in your task, of course.'

'Task?' breathed Nora.

'Why, yes, when you were making that request, you suggested that you needed help to find that invention of your ancestor, old Peter Lavery, together with proof that it was Peter who invented it. A very good idea, if I may say so. Righting two wrongs at the same time, do you see? The wrong to Peter himself, and the bit of encouragement to your Da that might make all the difference to him. So here I am, and I'll help in any way I can.'

Jik looked puzzled. Nora explained hurriedly.

'I lit a candle this morning, and I thought if we could find proof that a Lavery invented radar or whatever it was, then the Da might feel he had something to be proud of, and it might make him pull himself up, see?'

She said nothing about the light she had seen, and the voice.

Jik looked sceptical.

'Maybe,' he said. 'Or maybe not.'

Then he turned to The Snapper.

'I don't understand most of this,' he said politely, 'but thank you for your offer of help. Only I don't quite see what any of us can do, including you.'

The Snapper began to scowl again.

'No doubt you don't,' he said, and for the first time, Nora thought, it was definitely a snap. 'No doubt you don't. And is there some reason why you would expect to know everything, Jik, my lad?'

It was Jik's turn to blush. 'So, what can you do, then?' he muttered. 'We can't very well go back and see old Peter inventing his contraption, and get a signed statement from someone alive then as proof!'

'Oh, can't we?' asked The Snapper. 'Where and when would you like to go?'

Jik and Nora stared at him.

'You mean – like, time travel?' asked Jik in awe. 'Can you really take us back in time?'

'I can do much more than that,' boasted The Snapper genially. 'But if that's what you want, just name the time and I'm your man!'

'But don't you need a spaceship thingy?' asked Nora at last, memories of Dr Who flooding back. 'What would we travel in?'

'And what's wrong with the great boat you're standing in?' asked the old man, his blue eyes twinkling more brightly than ever. 'And you haven't invited me to come on board yet, I might remark.'

'Oh, yes, please come on board!' cried Nora.

'Both of you want me to?' asked The Snapper, looking ready to scowl again.

But Jik said at once, 'Yes, please come on board,' and the scowl went.

The Snapper swung himself deftly over the rail, and looked round him with pleasure.

'Well,' he said. 'This is more like it! It's years since I last set foot on the deck of a real light sailing vessel!'

He smiled at them both, and they smiled back, suddenly sure that whoever this strange sailor was, he was a friend.

'Now,' said The Snapper. 'Let's get down to business.'

# Chapter Seven

'The first thing,' said The Snapper, 'is to take her out into the open sea. Not too far out, mind. But we can't go anywhere while we're tied up, and we can't float about loose in the Marina, right?'

They nodded solemnly.

'So, how are you as sailors, then?' asked The Snapper.

'Jik's very good,' Nora said. 'The Da always said he was. The Da used to let him be captain sometimes, and the Da was crew, to let Jik get to know more about it.'

'Only twice,' said Jik honestly. 'And it was ages ago. I'd rather be crew, if you don't mind. And Nora knows quite a lot, too.'

'Good.' The Snapper regarded them with the twinkling eyes that were becoming so familiar. 'So I'll be captain, then? Well, it suits me better, I won't deny, for when a man has been captain it's hard to go back to being crew again. And have you thought where you want to go? In time, I mean?'

'Oh, but won't you tell us where would be best?' Nora asked anxiously, but The Snapper was shaking his head.

'No,' he said. 'I'm only here to help. The guts of the task is your own. Make a decision, and I'll take you there.'

'Ah, dear goodness,' sighed Nora. 'I wish I was better at history.'

'Well, we'll get the engine started, and the boat cast off, first,' said The Snapper. 'Then when we're out of the Marina we'll hoist the sails. That's the easier way, to my thinking. And when we're all set, you can tell me your decision.'

Jik and Nora nodded.

'Oh, and there's one thing,' The Snapper added. 'Since we're doing this time travelling under sail, we need to go from boat to boat.'

'What do you mean?' asked Jik.

'Well, if we were taking off from land, we could go anywhere on land, but since we're starting on the sea, we have to go back to the sea. You can go to any boat you like and stay on her, but once you set foot on land you'll find yourselves back in your own time, and on board the *Lady Molly* again.'

'Sure, that's okay,' said Jik impatiently. 'The Da always says, when he tells us the story, that old Peter was on board ship when he thought of his invention, so on a ship is where we need to be too, right?'

'That's right!' agreed Nora eagerly.

'Fair enough,' said The Snapper. 'No problem there, then. Just one thing. I won't be coming with you, you know. You'll have to learn to manage this on your own. Now, then, my hearties, all hands on deck! Jik, do you have a key for this engine of your Da's?'

Jik produced the key.

'We need a few minutes to warm her up,' Captain Snapper reminded them. 'I want you at the bow, Jik, and you at the stern, Nora, ready to cast off the mooring ropes when I give you the word.'

Jik and Nora sprang readily into position.

Then Nora turned back.

'You have the key of the main cabin there, Captain Snapper,' she said, 'and you'll need it to get out the Da's compass and his other instruments. He keeps them locked up in there.'

'Thanks, able seaman Nora,' said The Snapper gravely. 'I'll get them now.'

Five minutes later, they were steering carefully out between the red port markers and the green starboard markers, until they reached the entrance to the marina.

The day was still just as beautiful. The sun gleamed on the little wavelets, and *Lady Molly* bobbed happily along.

The Snapper seemed to be a skilful enough helmsman. He weaved his way dextrously past the other boats and between the markers. Soon they were looking around at open sea.

'Now,' said The Snapper, 'Nora, come and hold the helm for a while. Just keep her on a straight course for that buoy over there. Do you see it?'

Nora nodded.

'Good girl. Jik and I are going to put the sails up, but just you ignore us and concentrate on your own job. Can you do that, do you think?'

# Chapter 7

'I think so,' Nora said. 'The Da taught me to steer a good while ago, and I've done it quite often. Thought not recently,' she added. 'I think I should remember.'

'Okay. It won't take long to get the sails up, and then either Jik or I will relieve you.'

Nora stared straight ahead at the buoy. It was quite a long way off. Ireland's Eye, the big island, was over a bit to the left. To port, she quickly corrected herself. She gripped the wheel hard, trying to stick to the course. How awful if she went the wrong way!

Still, unless there are shallows or rocks to avoid, it isn't easy to go too far wrong at sea. She kept one eye on the buoy and one on the compass, and occasionally made slight adjustments to the wheel, and presently, to her delight, she found the skill coming back to her.

She relaxed her over tight grip on the wheel, and allowed herself to enjoy the pleasure of being at sea again.

Meanwhile Jik and The Snapper started to get the sails up, operating the roller reefing to open out the foresail. Colm had put in roller reefing for the jib to make life easier. The Snapper loosed off the jib sheet on the port side, holding it loosely, while Jik loosed the sheet on the starboard side. He wrapped it skillfully around the winch, then operated the winch energetically to unfurl the sail. The breeze filled the foresail immediately and the yacht began to lean over to starboard.

Then, at a nod from The Snapper, Jik hopped up onto the cabin roof to the mast and began to take the cover off the main sail, handing it to The Snapper to stow away in the cockpit. Nora had to keep moving from side to side to see past both Jik and the foresail.

*Lady Molly* was gaff rigged. Jik hesitated for a moment to work out which halyard operated the topping lift and reached it over to The Snapper to attach to the end of the gaff, to which the mainsail was attached. Then they hauled up the gaff, Jik pulling hard on the halyards, while The Snapper controlled the boom with the mainsheet, until the sail was fully in position. Then Jik made fast the halyards to the cleats on the mast.

Jik enjoyed himself showing his skills with the sails and with fastening ropes, and flushed with pleasure when The Snapper, although sharp enough to start with in his orders, ended by praising him.

'We'll make a sailor out of you yet, lad,' said The Snapper, and Jik grinned happily as, at another nod from The Snapper, he pulled the lever to switch off the engine.

They made their way back to Nora at the helm, and The Snapper said, 'Let's all relax for a minute, now. I'll take the helm, Nora, if you like, and you and Jik take a short while to make your minds up.'

# Chapter Eight

Nora and Jik looked at each other helplessly.

They perched themselves on the bench which ran around the cockpit, and for a moment or two said nothing.

'The thing is,' said Jik eventually, 'that we aren't too sure when exactly this inventing happened. We might need to have several goes at it before we get it right. Will that be okay, Snapper?'

'Only one go today,' said The Snapper briskly. 'But after that, we'll see. In a way, it will depend on how you behave this time.'

'Oh.'

What does he mean? wondered Jik, but was reluctant to ask.

'What do you mean?' asked Nora bluntly.

'Well, you're getting this chance because you, Nora, made an unselfish request, see? So if you want another chance, you'll have to do something else unselfish during your trip, right? Easy enough?'

He looked at them quizzically.

'Easy enough for Nora, I'd say,' he added. 'Don't know about you, young Jik. So you'd better try to get it right first time.'

There was a pause while they thought about it.

'Any ideas yet?' The Snapper asked presently.

'I'd like to go back to the days of the ancient kings of Ireland,' said Jik boldly. 'When there was a High King at Tara, and everyone had adventures all the time. That would be something like!'

'But, Jik!' Nora said anxiously, 'sure, that would be far too early in history, wouldn't it? I think we only need to go back three or four hundred years. Only I'm not really sure how many hundreds.'

'Ah, come on, Nora! When'll we ever get a chance like this again? Will you ever catch yourself on and get a life? You heard what he said. If it's the wrong time, we just have to do something unselfish and we'll get another go! Besides, the Da talked about 'the mists of time', so that sounds long enough ago, right?'

Nora stared at her brother's excited face. She was as sure as could be that he was asking for the wrong time. Jik just wanted to go exploring, he wasn't thinking about old Peter's invention, or about the Da.

For a moment she came near to losing her temper with him.

'Ah, let's do it, Nora!' he said. There was a pleading note in his voice.

Nora made up her mind. What decided it was the thought of the miserable time Jik had had over the past two years. They had both had a bad time, but somehow, Nora felt that it had been worse for Jik than for her.

This was something he really wanted. She couldn't be mean enough to put her foot down and refuse to agree.

'Well, Nora?' The Snapper's voice interrupted her thoughts. 'You both have to agree on the time, mind now! If you have another suggestion, make it and we'll see if Jik will give way to you.'

'No.' Nora drew a deep breath. 'No, that's okay, Jik. The ancient times, the times of the High Kings, it is. Right?'

'Good girl,' said The Snapper.

'But, hey!' Nora suddenly thought. 'Won't they all speak ancient Gaelic, or something? I mean, like, Jik and me know some Irish, all right. We're learning it at school. But I don't think …'

'We couldn't keep up much of a conversation in it, yet, she means,' supplied Jik.

'That's okay,' The Snapper said. 'It's one of the terms and conditions of time travel. You can make yourselves understood, and you can understand, what everybody says. And another thing, you'll be going outside time, so no time passes in this life, okay? Do you get it?'

'Oh, yes.' said Jik confidently.

'I think so,' said Nora.

'I mean,' explained The Snapper, 'Your Da won't even know you've been away. It'll be like no time has passed, to him, see?'

'Oh, right!' said Jik. 'Wow! We could be anywhere, for all he knows!'

'You'll be where I know you are!' growled The Snapper. 'And don't forget it! Behave yourselves, or I'll fetch you straight back, land or no land, and that'll be the end of it!'

He sounded, Jik thought, a bit like Ma when she was laying down the law. It had always been Ma who made sure they did as they were told. The Da had always been the easy-going one.

# Chapter 8

Nora didn't think of her mother, but she felt a warm comforting sense of security. The Snapper would see to it that they didn't do anything stupid.

'Now, my hearties,' he went on, 'you'd do well to stand up, and look respectful. Remember, you'll be going where cheek isn't appreciated. The people you'll meet are the word and a blow type. One word out of turn and they might have knocked you down before you'd finished speaking …'

'So, the school playground all over again?' murmured Jik, with a grin to Nora.

But The Snapper was not amused.

'I'm warning you for your own good,' he growled. 'But Mister Jik knows it all already, right? Yeah, the school playground, if they carry swords and daggers there!'

'Well … maybe not swords, but Charlie Flanagan has a pretty big flick knife … okay, okay,' he added hastily, seeing the look on The Snapper's face. 'Thanks for the warning. We'll be careful!'

The Snapper growled softly to himself, but said no more.

'If you're ready, then, my hearties, hold on to your hats!'

'We aren't wearing hats, Snapper …' began Nora innocently, then she was silent.

There was a loud, ominous creaking from the sails.

Nora looked round her. Was she imagining it, or had everything suddenly grown darker?

A whirl of black clouds scudded across the sky, and a fierce cold wind pulled her hair loose from its clasp and whirled it about her face. Nora put her hands up to push the hair out of her eyes.

'Wow!' said Jik.

Nora knew he had shouted, but she could hardly hear him. His voice was faint against the creaking of the ropes and the flapping of the sails as the mast swayed in the sudden gale.

She felt herself staggering as the *Lady Molly* began bucketing about in the wild lashing of the waves.

Seizing the grab rail she collapsed onto the bench behind her, and heard her own voice crying out, 'Snapper! Help!'

Jik, flung across the cockpit by a quick lurch sideways from the boat, landed on her knee, panting breathlessly.

'Wow!' he said again.

Unbelievingly, Nora realised that he was enjoying this.

He was mad!

They were both mad!

What did The Snapper mean by bringing them into this? He should have warned them!

She heard a soft laugh near her ear, and realised it was The Snapper. He smiled briefly at her, showing bright white teeth against his tanned skin.

'Hold on tight!' he roared. 'Nearly there!'

Then, abruptly, the noise of the gale died away, the boat settled down, and Nora was able to breathe again.

Strangely, though, it was still dark, although it should be the middle of a July afternoon.

But Nora had no time to wonder about that.

A hand seized her roughly by the arm, pulled her to her feet.

A voice spoke into her face.

'Ha! What have we here? Stowaways, by my oath! Speak! Who are you, and what do you want with me, aboard the *White Lady?*'

Nora, trembling with horror, could say nothing.

# Chapter Nine

It was Jik who first found his voice.

'We are not stowaways. Let go of my sister's arm!'

To his surprise, the stranger immediately released Nora's arm, stepped back, and bowed.

'Your pardon, lady. In the dark, I did not see at first that you were a woman. Nevertheless, my question remains.'

'We are travellers,' said Jik. He thought desperately. 'We did not expect to arrive on your boat, whoever you are. We were on our own boat at first, but in the storm it has disappeared. I am Jik and this is my sister Nora.' He attempted a bow, not nearly as gracefully as the other.

'I am Setanta,' replied the young man instantly. 'My courtesy requires that I should welcome strangers, especially strangers in distress. It would have been easier for me to abide by my training in this if you had called for help to come aboard, instead of climbing, as I suppose, up the stern? It is good to welcome strangers, but it is foolish to allow enemies to creep up unawares. And I have had many attacks and adventures already on this voyage.'

'It all happened so quickly that there was no time to call out,' apologised Jik.

'Come, let me take you to my cabin and show you hospitality,' said Setanta. 'This way.'

He ushered them before him to a low flight of steps, leading downwards to a cabin lit by some sort of lantern. In the beam of light thrown out unto the steps, they saw that he was a slight, dark young man, perhaps fifteen or sixteen, with a wiry, muscular strength about him in spite of his youth and size.

They went in, blinking in the sudden light, and stooping, for the entrance was low even for them. How grown ups got in at all was a mystery to Nora.

A tall, fair-haired boy stood up from the table as they appeared. Nora looked at him.

Her mouth dropped open.

It must be her imagination, sure.

But this boy seemed so familiar. She could almost have addressed him as Sean.

No, sure it had to be just a chance resemblance.

She almost missed his first words, as he spoke to Setanta.

'Ah, little hound, what catch from your hunting is this?'

'Peace, Laeg,' said Setanta, laughing. 'These are friends, I swear, not captives. Their boat has been lost in the storm, and they seek refuge and help, which we must gladly offer.'

Laeg swept a bow.

'Come, be seated,' he invited. 'There is wine and bread and meat here in plenty.'

Nora found, to her embarrassment, that both young men, or boys, for after all they were only a year or two older than Jik, were staring at her.

She remembered that she was, as usual, wearing jeans. Perhaps girls didn't wear jeans in this ancient time?

'But tell me, then, Hound Cub,' went on Laeg, 'who are these new friends you have found?'

Setanta laughed again.

'In truth, Laeg,' he said, 'I would do better to allow them to introduce themselves. For their names are outlandish, and I would sound foolish both to them and to you if I tried to repeat them on one hearing.'

Jik realised that both boys were looking at him.

'I am Jik,' he said, in his polite telephone voice, for he could see that his normal speech to equals was not going to work in this atmosphere of extreme courtesy. 'And this lady is my sister, Nora.'

The boys hesitated to speak.

'And of what clan are my friends Jik and Nora?' asked Setanta after a short pause.

'Of the clan of Lavery.' Jik hoped he was getting this right.

'Indeed, a clan respected throughout Ulster,' Setanta replied.

'But …' Laeg spoke again. 'This … lady. Does the clan of Lavery dress its women in men's clothing?'

'Only when its women take part in warfare, Laeg.'

It was Nora who spoke, for the first time. What made her say what she did, she was not sure, but it seemed, to her relief, to be accepted.

## Chapter 9

'And what warfare do you plan to wage, Lady Nora?' asked Setanta.

'We are going to right a wrong,' Jik said.

He looked at Laeg and Setanta, and smiled nervously.

'It's like this, right? Our great great great grandfather made a valuable discovery which can help to save sailors' lives. But no one believes that he had any part in inventing it. We want to find proof, and take it back with us.'

The boys looked interested.

'A useful discovery, I think,' said Setanta. 'Tell us more about it.'

'It helps to steer ships in fog and mist,' said Nora, 'when it's too murky to see by the stars. At least, I think it's something like that.'

'A wonderful thing, indeed,' said Laeg gravely. 'But, alas, I can be of little help to you here, for I have never heard of such an object.' He laughed. 'Many a night, I would have been glad to know of it, indeed!'

'It may be that our captain will know more,' said Setanta. 'When we have supped, I will take you to speak with him. But now, it is time to break our fast, and here is food if you will accept it?'

# Chapter Ten

They sat round the plain wooden table, and passed each other the horn of wine and chunks of bread and meat.

Laeg took a dagger from his belt and politely cut a chunk of bread from the loaf and offered it to Nora.

Setanta laughed.

'Well, you are greatly honoured, Lady Nora! That is Laeg's special dagger, once owned by the wonder working Druid, Bantha, and never to be used on any except holy or very important occasions!'

'And what could be more holy or important than to offer bread to my lady Nora?' Laeg replied. He spoke in a chaffing tone, and Nora wasn't sure at first if he was joking or serious. Until she caught his eye.

There was no doubt that he meant it.

Nora lowered her own eyes, and realised that once again she was blushing.

She took the bread, her fingers touching his, and whispered, her voice sounding unnaturally hoarse, 'Thanks, Laeg.'

Laeg wiped the dagger on his tunic, and carefully returned it to its place at his belt.

Nora and Jik realised that they were ravenously hungry.

Whether it was the excitement, or the cold during the storm, or just the fact that they had eaten nothing much since breakfast time, they were suddenly ready to eat anything they were offered.

There was a strong cheese, a type of meat which seemed a bit like corned beef, though they knew it couldn't be, the rough but very satisfying bread, and an even rougher wine, which Nora, after one gulp, found undrinkable, but which Jik swilled down with the others.

Noticing her reaction to the wine, Laeg kindly fetched Nora some water, which she drank instead with relief.

At last, they had finished most of the food in sight, and all four leaned back luxuriously, with a feeling of complete satisfaction.

'So, do you intend to fight for your family rights, my bold heroes?' asked Setanta.

'If we have to,' flashed Jik, and Nora nodded her head vigorously.

'My father needs to have his rights,' she said, rather fiercely.

'A small warrior, by my oath, but a brave one!' exclaimed Setanta. 'It seems that the women warriors begin to outnumber the men. Queen Maeve, and the Princess Aifa, and Skatha. It is Skatha whom I seek. Skatha is said to be the source of all the greatest wisdom in the arts of war. I go to seek her in the land of Shadows where she lives, to entreat her to teach me all she knows. And now, here is the prettiest female warrior of them all, by my life!'

Nora blushed furiously.

But before she could say anything, Jik burst out, 'Wow, I know who you are!'

He turned to Nora.

'Setanta! But Laeg calls him little hound! And he's on his way to learn the arts of war from Skatha! Don't you see? Remember the 'Tales and Legends of Ireland' the Da read to us last winter?'

Light burst on Nora. She exclaimed, 'You're Cuchulain!'

'Indeed, little lady, so I have been called, Cullen's hound. You know the story?'

'Everyone knows the story!' interjected Laeg. 'But probably they don't know that when King Conor called you to go with him to feast at the Dun of Cullen the Swordsmith, you excused yourself, and promised to catch him up, just because you were playing hurley, and were afraid that our team would loose without your skill! And yet it was I, not you, who scored the winning goal!'

He punched Cuchulain lightly on the shoulder, and Cuchulain laughed.

'You speak the truth,' he acknowledged. 'But how was I to expect that, going by your usual form?'

He dodged another punch from Laeg.

'So the result was, I was late arriving at Cullen's Dun. King Conor and his warriors were feasting within, and the gates were barricaded, as was done each night, by high and heavy thorn bushes. Worse than that, Cullen's mighty wolfhound, whom he loved like a son, had been let loose as a further guard, and as I pulled aside the barricade and tried to enter the court, he leapt at me out of nowhere, his teeth not an inch from my throat.'

'Wow!' sighed Jik.

'I had little choice. I looked around me for aid. There was none to be seen.

'Swiftly I drew my sword. I thrust my sword through his throat.

'He dropped to the ground lifeless.

'I slew Cullen's mighty guard dog, before he could slay me.'

Cuchulain looked down at the table, and they saw his lip quiver. 'It was an evil deed, for Cullen loved the hound, and if I had not been late in coming, I would have been safely inside before the beast was set loose to guard the court.

'So I offered myself to Cullen, to take the place of his wolf-hound and guard his court for as long as need be.'

Then he looked up, and laughed again.

'But Cullen forgave me the wrong, and released me from my offer. And he prophesied that one day I would be the guard dog of all Ulster.

'And so Fergus Mac Roy said, 'Let us call him Cuchulain, the Hound of Cullen, after this first battle of his!'

'And so it has been, until many have forgotten my real name, Setanta!'

'I should have known at once when Laeg called you 'little hound',' said Jik.

'Ah,' said Cuchulain, 'not many are permitted to call me little, or cub, as this bold rascal does. But Laeg is my charioteer, a boy of equal birth with my own, and therefore not one who would normally take on that task, but I chose him and he came willingly, and has rights and privileges as my faithful friend which few are allowed.' He frowned fiercely.

'What would you do if anyone else called you 'little hound'?' ventured Nora.

'What would I do? Deal with the villain in a way not fit for a lady's ears, bold warrior though she may be.' Cuchulain smiled sadly. 'Though, in truth, there are a few other friends who might call me so and live. And, indeed, it was by that name – Little Hound – that my lady Emer addressed me, when she bade me go and become a man before I sought her again as my wife.'

'Sure, are you not far too young yet to be married?' asked Jik.

'Why so?' frowned Cuchulain. 'I was thought young to Take Valour – that is, to become a full warrior – but that was more than a year ago, and since then I have proved my manhood in battle. To everyone but the lady Emer, it seems. When I return to her, with the skills Skatha will teach me, I will be a man indeed. But, truly, there are more ways than one to become a man, and Emer may in her jealousy regret her words, when she sees me become a man in other ways, and know the beauty of other women than herself.'

'Oh, don't, don't!' Nora exclaimed. 'I know what you're thinking. But you mustn't! You love Emer. If you don't stay faithful to her, you'll end up bringing one of the biggest sorrows of your life on you! Oh, please don't!'

'What, are you a priestess of the Druids as well as a warrior, little maiden?' laughed Cuchulain. 'Can you see into the future?'

'No, I'm certainly nothing to do with the Druids,' said Nora earnestly. 'I can't explain, but please believe that I know what I'm saying. You have to make your own choice, I know that, but you don't have to make the wrong one, do you?'

Cuchulain looked puzzled. 'You remind me of my lady Emer, little Nora,' he said abruptly. 'Your dark hair, your white skin, your blue eyes. You are younger than Emer, I would guess, by some few years, but in a short enough time you, like Emer, will have the power to draw men's hearts from their bosoms. There,' he laughed again suddenly, 'a prophesy for you, to match yours to me.'

He was interrupted by a scream from the upper deck, a hoarse cry sounding a note of panic

'Help! Man overboard!'

# Chapter Eleven

For a moment they froze.

Then, quicker than Nora could have believed possible, Cuchulain was bounding up the steps to the cockpit, and seconds later she, Laeg, and Jik, were following at their best speed.

There was no time to waste.

A sailor, probably the one who had shouted, stood in the bows of the ship peering desperately over the port side, a torch – a flaming stick – held high in his hand. The beams of light flashed over the waves as they lashed against the ship, but there seemed at first nothing to be seen.

Then a shout burst simultaneously from Nora and Laeg, 'There!'

They could just see an arm which rose above the waves and then was lost to sight again. Nora, remembering the times when they had practised for just this sort of emergency, kept her eyes fixed on the stark, white face just visible against the blackness of the sea, and began to point in the right direction. It was essential, she knew, for one person to do this, and to keep doing this, until someone else reached the drowning man.

Suddenly, peering into the faint light cast in the darkness by the torch, she stiffened.

Surely – or was she imagining it? – surely there was a second man struggling in the waves?

Jik shouted to the helmsman, 'Take her back, can't you? Tack into the wind! When you get back to the spot, turn her head on into the wind and hold her steady!'

As Jik spoke, Cuchulain leapt onto the edge of the side deck, and a moment later had dived into the darkness.

'Wait, wait!' cried Jik in vain. The boy had gone almost before he had time to speak.

'The fool!' Jik burst out. 'Why didn't he wait for a life belt?'

'What do you mean?' asked Laeg furiously. 'Don't call my lord Cuchulain a fool! He is the bravest person I've ever known!'

'The Da always says that at sea, you need to be bright as well as brave!' retorted Jik. 'Well, if you've never heard of a life-belt, then at least you've heard of a rope! Has anyone got one?'

Another sailor, listening intently, hurried forward with a stout coil, and Jik lost no time in tying it round his waist.

'And any pieces of wood you can find. Decent sized ones, right?'

Laeg dived back into the cabin and returned almost at once with two broad planks which, Nora thought, probably helped to turn the table into a double bunk when necessary.

'Chuck them over!' ordered Jik briefly.

It was funny, thought Nora, how everyone was listening to Jik and obeying him.

He was like the Da in that way. People accepted what he said, and did as he told them, because he so clearly knew what he was talking about.

Jik gave a final tug at the other end of the rope, which he had lashed to the port bulwark, and went over the side without another word.

Already, although only seconds had passed since Cuchulain's dive, it seemed too late.

But then Nora realised that the helmsman, who must be the captain, she thought, had swung the ship round, while Jik was giving his instructions, and tacked back into the wind.

Instead of moving at full speed away from the spot where the man had gone overboard, they were now hove-to quite nearby.

When Jik jumped, they were as near to the scene of the accident as possible.

As the sailor with the flaming torch held it high overhead, she could see that Cuchulain had reached the man and was supporting him as far above the waves as he could. And, yes, there was another person there, hanging on to the first, a pale face only just to be seen, washed over moment by moment by the waves.

Cuchulain was struggling desperately to retain some sort of hold on both men.

As she watched in horror, she saw Jik pushing the wooden planks ahead of him, like the pieces of polystyrene they used in life saving class. He had nearly reached the others, and although she could hear no words above the sound of the wind, he was clearly giving Cuchulain instructions, for a moment later Cuchulain was resting some of his weight on one of the planks, and pushing both men's arms over the other one.

Then Jik began to haul on the rope, and Cuchulain took hold of it with one hand, while with the other he still held the nearly drowned men over the plank, and together Jik and Cuchulain, holding onto the men and to the rope as best as they could, began to move towards the ship.

'Pull the rope!' ordered Nora fiercely.

Laeg, understanding first, seized the rope at the end tied to the side of the ship, as Nora tried, without much success, to haul it in. The two sailors joined in.

Nora allowed them to take her place at the rope. Instead, she seized the torch and continued to direct its flaring light to the four struggling in the sea.

Suddenly it was over. Jik and Cuchulain were hoisting the men, almost a dead weight, over the side onto the deck, and a moment later were climbing aboard themselves, helped by eager hands.

Then they were all four wrapped in warm blankets, and were hurried down to the main cabin to be given hot wine and dry clothes.

The whole operation had taken less than ten minutes.

'But what happened?' asked Nora, when three of the sea-logged people were seated in the main cabin and no longer shivering quite so much. The fourth, the stranger, lay still barely conscious on the bunk to one side, while Laeg held a cup of wine to his lips.

'My fault, lady,' said the crew member who had been rescued. He was a tall, dark haired man, with the typical tanned face of sailors and outdoors men. 'I was keeping a lookout ahead, and thought I saw a sail. Then there was a splash, and I saw this man struggling in the water. I leaned forward to see better, the waves drove hard and the ship rocked more than usual, and I was gone.'

'And was there a sail?' inquired Cuchulain eagerly.

'I think so, my lord,' answered the sailor, 'but if so it must have been moving away, for as you see there's no sign of it now. So it's no longer a danger.'

'A danger?' asked Jik in surprise.

'Aye. These seas are alive with pirates, didn't you know?'

Jik and Nora shook their heads in surprise.

'This man must have been thrown over board,' Laeg explained to them. 'Very likely the ship he was travelling on was captured and sunk, any valuables stolen, and those who were left alive tied up, like this man, and heaved overboard to drown. And, look!

The blanket wrapped round him hid the ropes from me at first, but you can see now, he has been tied up!'

Jik and Nora saw in horror that ropes were indeed tied tightly round the man's arms and body.

Laeg tugged in vain at the sodden knots, then, with an impatient exclamation, pulled out his dagger and slashed the ropes apart.

'This action, releasing a prisoner nearly drowned, is also in my eyes significant and holy!' he muttered.

As he wiped the blade and returned the dagger to its place at his waist, he failed to notice the eyes of the rescued stranger had opened, and were fastened on Laeg's dagger with an expression of terror. If anyone had been looking, they would have seen the look in the stranger's eyes change almost at once to a baleful mixture of anger and hatred.

'But,' said Nora presently, 'what I don't understand is why it took two of you to rescue the sailor. Can't he swim? And why did the other sailors do nothing?'

Laeg stared at her. 'None of the sailors can swim, Nora. For that matter, neither can I. Cuchulain is the only one among us who has the skill. And, of course,' he bowed to Jik, 'you, my lord Jik.'

'Then,' said Nora vigorously, 'It's about time you all learnt! It's stupid to be out on a boat and not be able to swim.'

'And so say I, Nora,' smiled Cuchulain. 'But the sailors are superstitious, and think otherwise, and apart from myself, most of the king's warriors are seldom near water, and see no need.'

'But,' said Laeg, 'if you, Lady Nora, will teach me, I will gladly learn.' And he smiled at Nora in a way which made her suddenly lower her eyes, and begin to blush again.

'Now,' said Cuchulain, 'you have done much for us. It behoves us to repay your help as best we can. Jik, you spoke of an invention of your ancestor, and I promised that our captain would give what help he could out of his long years of seafaring knowledge. I would have offered this in any case, but now it is offered with a full heart. I hope your task will prosper.'

Jik and Nora began to thank him, but he would have none of it.

'Nevertheless,' he added, 'it is my thought that for now you should rest, and early on the morrow, when my captain comes off watch and is freer to talk, I will take you to him.'

It seemed a good idea. They were both yawning, and bed had seldom seemed so attractive.

## Chapter 11

Nora was led away to a small cabin under the bows, where a single bunk with a rough warm blanket smiled at her invitingly, and Jik was offered a share in the sleeping quarters in the main cabin with Laeg and Cuchulain, which pleased him greatly.

They slept soundly. The rocking of the boat, and the sound of the wind, were no more than a lullaby.

# Chapter Twelve

In the morning, the sun shining through the portholes woke them both.

The sea seemed calmer. Jik, shown the heads by the other boys, came to knock Nora up and show her in turn where to wash. He found her up and pulling on her jeans.

'A bit primitive,' he warned her, 'but okay.'

'All boats are primitive,' Nora said reasonably. 'What would you expect? But, goodness, Jik, why does it roll so much, even now the storm's over?'

'Oh, the Da told me about that once,' began Jik instructively. 'Old boats didn't have proper deep keels like a modern day yacht, just a small keel and a lot of ballast in the centre. See, the deep keel, like on *Lady Molly*, acts like a sort of brake against the waves to keep her steady –'

But Nora, grinning, had disappeared in the direction of the heads.

Shortly afterwards, they wandered out on to the deck, and found Laeg and Cuchulain in serious conversation with the captain.

'Ah, good morrow, my friends,' Cuchulain greeted them. 'Sleep well? Good. Breakfast in the main cabin. This is Captain Forgall, who will happily serve you in whatever way you ask. I have spoken to him of your quest.'

'Morning, my masters,' said the captain briskly. 'When you've breakfasted, you'll find me on the foredeck. I'll be happy to give you any help I can.'

By daylight, they were able to get a better idea of the ship. As they shared the bread and wine, or in Nora's case, water, in the cabin, they commented on its size.

'Not much bigger than *Lady Molly*,' said Nora, munching hungrily.

'Well, about half as big again, I'd say,' Jik corrected her. 'But still, smaller than lots of the boats in the Marina. Not very safe for seas like these, right?'

But the captain, when they joined him on the foredeck, spoke of the vessel in tones of pride, and it was clear that he thought of her as one of the finest and largest ships afloat on those seas. They noticed that he did not call her a boat, but always referred to her as a ship.

She had, he boasted, a crew of three hands as well as himself, and had sailed the coasts of Ireland in all weathers. She had carried as many as five passengers, and among these, famous warriors and kings.

Jik and Nora were glad they had said nothing about the size of the vessel, but had only remarked on the change in the weather this morning, and the smoothness of the ship's motion. They were careful to say ship, rather than boat.

When the captain had finally finished telling them about his pride and joy, Jik ventured to turn the conversation to Peter Lavery's invention.

'Something to help sail in the fog and murk?' repeated the captain. 'Ha, I would give much for such a thing! Too often, the sun by day or the stars by night are hidden, and we must drop anchor and wait for clear skies.'

'Of course, you can always use your compass when you have a safe, known route, without too many shallows and rocks,' Nora was beginning, but the captain interrupted her. His long melancholy face took on an expression of the utmost surprise.

'Compass? What's that?'

Jik and Nora looked at each other.

'Why, a compass has a needle which always points due north,' Nora began. 'Sure, you'll have seen one many a time?'

'Compass?' repeated the captain. 'Indeed, I have heard that in the barbarian lands beyond the seas such things are known, but by my life I, who have sailed these seas thirty years, have never seen one. I had thought it a wild travellers' tale, or perhaps a forbidden magic. Tell me more about this compass!'

'I'll do better than tell you, I'll show you,' Jik promised, diving into his hip pocket. 'I brought it with me because we were going to our boat. Though we had the Da's big compass, of course, but I like to have my own pocket one with me.'

The captain took it eagerly in one hand and listened carefully as Jik explained how the compass worked.

'By my life!' he exclaimed again 'With such a thing, we need never go astray! And this is an invention of your ancestor, you say?'

'No, no, that's been around for years,' Jik told him. 'Peter Lavery invented something even better, that shows up other ships or rocks or things in the way. You could only steer by compass if you had a clear chart of your route already, and even then you'd run the risk of bashing into another ship, or an iceberg like the Titanic did, or something.'

The captain looked puzzled. Clearly he had understood very little of what Jik had said.

He held the compass carefully in both hands now, and on his face was an expression of longing.

Nora had a sudden idea.

'Jik!' she said, 'Come here a minute.'

They moved to the side of the foredeck, while the captain still examined the compass.

'Couldn't we give it to him, or even to Cuchulain, as a present? They've been very kind to us, after all?'

'Hey, whose compass is it?' asked Jik indignantly.

'I'll buy you another one when we get home,' offered Nora.

'Well. Well, okay, then. Whatever. I'd like to give Cuchulain something, right? Like, meeting him is really something.'

Jik's brow cleared, and it was with a smiling face that he turned back to the captain and said, 'If you like, we will make a gift of this compass to Cuchulain, so that when he travels by ship you will always be able to take him safely on the right course.'

The captain's face lit up.

'It should stay on board my ship,' he bargained quickly, 'for of what use to Cuchulain would it be on land?'

'It's all the same, isn't it?' asked Nora innocently. 'Since this is his ship.'

'His ship?' cried the captain indignantly. 'No, indeed, this ship is mine, and let no one say other! But see, here he comes. Show him the gift, and I will ask him to let it remain on board, and in return he will have free passage from the *White Lady* ever after.'

Cuchulain was indeed bounding up the couple of steps to the foredeck.

'Land!' he cried. 'Captain, we can see land to starboard!'

'Good!' said Captain Forgall briskly. 'But meanwhile, see this gift which the strangers have made to you and me, Cuchulain, in return for their voyage.'

He thrust the compass towards Cuchulain, and began to explain what it was.

'The gift is to yourself, lord Cuchulain,' said Jik. 'But if you see fit to leave it on board this ship, it will be of use more often, and the captain offers you free transport from now on in return for this arrangement.'

'A good bargain! Jik, Nora, I thank you from my heart! Your generosity will not go unrewarded. When we are safely on land, I will choose some of my finest weapons to give you in return!' exclaimed Cuchulain. 'But now, captain, since land is approaching rapidly, do you need to direct your crew?'

A moment later, Jik and Nora were alone on the foredeck, as the captain and Cuchulain bustled off.

Land was indeed drawing near.

Suddenly both Jik and Nora remembered The Snapper's words.

They were about to touch land. The first foot on shore, and they would find themselves back home!

Laeg! thought Nora.

She rushed towards the cabin, hoping to see him in time to say goodbye.

Suddenly she heard shouts, sounds of a fierce struggle.

Nora tumbled down the steps head first, dragging the cabin door open. Inside to her horror she saw the stranger who had been rescued the night before spring on Laeg with a roar of anger. Nora screamed. What was happening?

The stranger had begun to wrestle with Laeg, and Nora saw that he was trying to drag the dagger from Laeg's belt. He was a large, thickset man, clearly much stronger than the boy, though not, perhaps, so skilled in the arts of hand to hand fighting, for as Nora watched, Laeg's foot went out and the man was sent sprawling.

'Help! Help! Cuchulain!' Nora shrieked 'Jik!'

Footsteps came thudding along the deck to her rear.

She darted aside, to allow Cuchulain room to squeeze past. Jik, also arriving, grabbed her arm. 'What's going on?' he shouted.

Nora saw out of the corner of her eye the rescued stranger seize Laeg by the ankle, pull him brutally to the floor, and immediately leap on top of him, his weight and strength allowing him to keep

# Chapter 12

Laeg pinned down. She turned back swiftly, saw the man's raised fist about to drive into Laeg's throat, and saw Cuchulain spring forward.

And just at that most frightening moment, the sky over Nora's head grew dark again, and the ship began to shake and shudder beneath her feet.

They hadn't set foot on shore, yet.

But apparently the magic worked slightly in advance of that.

Jik and Nora, unable to move, clung helplessly to each other, and to whatever parts of the ship they could reach.

The darkness grew thick.

The noise of the wind and the waves grew louder.

'Oh, why does time travel always have to be like this?' wailed Nora, sitting down suddenly on the jolting deck.

The darkness and noise reached their climax.

Then, suddenly, all was calm and peace again.

The sun was shining. There was no wind, but instead a gentle breeze. They were back on board the *Lady Molly*, and it seemed that The Snapper had brought her safely back to her berth in the Marina.

But what, Nora thought, her eyes full of tears, was happening to Laeg?

It seemed impossible to do anything now to help him.

# Chapter Thirteen

They reached home just in time.

The Da was coming out into the garden.

They heard his voice calling, 'Jik! Nora! Are you there, kids?'

It was time to eat.

'How's about we go into the city and eat out, lads?' asked Colm jovially. 'MacDonald's, Pizza Hut, whatever? Sure, we're owed a treat, right?'

'MacDonald's,' said Nora quickly. 'We had pizza last night.'

Apparently, Daddy hadn't noticed that they had been away for nearly twenty four hours. The time factor seemed to work, then.

'Right!' said Colm, in his cheery, 'getting on with the kids' voice. Then he paused. 'You know, lads, Pizza Hut doesn't just do pizzas. They have quite a range of other stuff.'

Nora's heart sank. She knew what that meant. Pizza Hut did wine and beer. Memories of the last time the Da had taken them there came flooding back. She couldn't bear a repeat performance of the Da's behaviour then.

'Or, even, what about the *Bad Ass?*' suggested Colm. 'A real, grown up night out, right? Time you had a special treat.'

It sounded good, even with the worry and questioning that flooded through Nora's mind. Had Cuchulain been able to pull the stranger off Laeg and rescue him? Had the rest of the crewmen been in time to help?

If only she could get hold of The Snapper and find out from him if Laeg was okay!

Maybe tomorrow they could find him and work something out?

Nora put her fears to one side, and ran upstairs to dress up for the special occasion in a short skirt and fancy top. She put on her new lipstick. The Da wouldn't notice, or at least not until it was too late. She considered blusher, but remembered what Cuchulain had said about her white skin, and decided not to.

Even Jik changed out of his T-shirt into an nice dark blue shirt with collar and long sleeves, and Colm shaved specially.

They drove into the centre of Dublin, parked at Stephen's Green, and walked towards Templebar.

It was then that things began to go wrong.

They were nearly there when Colm's mobile went off.

They could hear the Irish jig of his personalised ring tone. Nora listened and hoped he wouldn't hear.

However, it was no use.

'Just a minute, lads,' said Colm. He walked on ahead of them and listened, then spoke.

They waited in resignation.

But for a moment, everything seemed to be fine.

'Come on, lads,' said Colm, shutting down his phone. 'Nearly there!'

Nora and Jik smiled at each other. They had expected that Colm would have told them that he had to forget about their evening out – that something else had come up. But it seemed that that wasn't happening.

Then catastrophe.

Walking towards them, smiling and confident, was a woman.

'Well, well, what a gas!' exclaimed Colm. 'This is my friend, Bridie Gallagher. You've heard me mention her, haven't you?'

Jik and Nora mumbled something in turn.

'Great to see you, Bridie!' Colm said heartily. 'We're just going for a meal at the *Bad Ass*. Have you eaten? Why don't you join us?'

'Why, thanks, Colm!' beamed the enemy. 'No, I haven't eaten yet. That'd be great!'

'Okay, kids?' said Colm.

'Brill,' said Jik with a stony face.

Nora said nothing.

They walked on towards the *Bad Ass Café*.

Both Jik and Nora were very well aware that they had been conned.

They got through the evening somehow.

To their surprise, Colm drank less than they had expected, and several times, when he was about to have another drink, Bridie Gallagher was the one who stopped him and made him change to a non-alcoholic beverage.

'Cool top, Nora,' Bridie said, when they were all sitting round the table and eating the complimentary garlic bread and coleslaw before the order arrived.

## Chapter 13

'Thanks,' mumbled Nora.

'Like the lipstick, too,' Bridie went on.

'Lipstick?' Colm said sharply.

Stupid cow! thought Nora, drawing the Da's attention to it!

But Bridie glared at Colm, and he shut up.

'What are you, nearly thirteen?' Bridie went on. 'I suppose I was round about that myself when I started wearing make-up. You look really cool tonight. Sweet.'

Nora couldn't help being a bit pleased.

Then the food arrived, and they all had something to do besides talk.

It was Jik who really noticed that Bridie, under her confident appearance, was nearly as nervous as the Da.

It was the first time they had really seen her. Colm had mentioned her name a lot, when making excuses for being out so much at night.

At first she had been one of the group.

Lately, however, there had been more and more mentions of 'Bridie' without other names attached.

For some reason, Jik had expected her to be big and blonde, with one of those busts that comics made jokes about.

Actually, she was small, slim, and nearly as dark-haired as Nora.

'So, Jik,' was her next attempt, 'I guess you miss getting down to the boat? Your Dad tells me you're a fine sailor!'

Jik went scarlet.

She couldn't know, could she?

No, of course not. It was just conversation.

'Yeah, I suppose,' he said.

Bridie was silent.

Thinking of something else to say, Jik supposed.

Suddenly he felt sorry for her.

'The Da's a great sailor,' he said. 'Really cool. You should get him to take you out some time.'

He felt Nora's glare scorching his left cheek.

'Hey, cool idea!' said Colm quickly. 'Let's all go out sometime soon. Weekend, it would have to be, because Bridie's a working girl, right, babe?'

'What do you work at, Bridie?' Jik asked.

He knew Nora was annoyed with him, but it was hard not to be polite, especially when the poor cow seemed more scared of them than anything else.

'I'm a computer programmer,' Bridie said.

Nora felt her mouth drop open.

'That's more Nora's style than mine,' Jik said. 'She's one of these computer whiz kids, got @ signs for eyeballs!'

Everyone laughed.

'Sounds like me when I was a teenager like you,' Bridie said. 'All my mates were out having fun knocking over bins and getting chased by the Garda, and I was stuck in front of the screen, hacking away. 'Would you ever leave off hammering that keyboard and get yourself out in the fresh air, Bridie!' my Mum used to say!'

She waited hopefully for Nora to respond, but there was silence.

Then Colm said quickly, 'Now, who's for a pudding?' and the moment passed.

It was over at last. The Da drove them home.

'Now, you need to get to bed in good time,' he said. 'You're not babies. You know how to look after yourselves. I'm going to run Bridie home, and when I get back, I expect to find you both asleep, right?'

'Right,' said Jik dryly. At about two o'clock, if we're lucky, he added silently to himself.

'You weren't very nice to the poor cow,' he said to Nora when the Da had gone.

'Why should I be?' asked Nora fiercely. 'She's caused us nothing but trouble, dragging the Da out every night and getting him drunk. Anyway, you were all over her, wasn't that enough?'

'I was just being friendly,' Jik said reasonably. 'Besides, I don't reckon anyone gets the Da drunk except himself.'

By agreement they dropped the subject.

# Chapter Fourteen

Next morning, Nora woke up full of ideas.

She wasn't sure what time the Da had got to bed, but she knew it had been late.

However, at least he hadn't fallen down the stairs and needed to be helped up again by Jik and herself.

'Hey, Jik!' she greeted him, when he wandered into the kitchen, yawning. 'Do you reckon we can get hold of The Snapper today? I really want to find out what happened to Laeg. Yeah, and we should try to have some idea where we want him to take us, right? How would it be if we took a look at the library, this morning? Try to work out where would be a good place to go next?'

'Go?' said Jik sourly. 'Come on, what makes you think we'll be going anywhere? We were supposed to do an unselfish deed, remember, if we wanted another chance.'

Nora couldn't help laughing.

'Hey, I guess we did more than one!' she smiled. 'Well, you did, anyway. We helped to rescue those guys, especially you, and then you gave your compass to the captain. I should think The Snapper would say that was plenty. I'm not so sure about me, though,' she added with a worried frown, 'though I did help a bit with the rescue, but not as much as you.'

Jik brightened up.

'You think that would count? Cool! I never even thought about it at the time. Well, if it counts for me, it counts for you as well. Remember you promised to buy me a new compass? That's unselfish, right?'

'I suppose so.' Nora felt a twinge of regret at the rash promise she had made. She had been saving up for a proper manicure set with eyebrow tweezers. Well, it would just have to wait.

'So, what about the library?'

'Yeah, cool. And you can buy me the compass on the way.'

They headed for the city centre.

The library had plenty of reference books, they knew.

They had used it before, for school projects.

It should be able to tell them where to aim for.

When they reached the library, they headed straight for the reference section.

It was full of Children's Encyclopaedias, and Histories of Inventions, and so on.

On a bright summer afternoon, there were very few other people there.

'Maybe we should ask the Librarian for some help?' Jik suggested.

Followed by Nora, he went up to the desk.

The Librarian was a tall, grim faced woman with straggly grey hair.

'Well, children?'

They cringed. No one called them children any more. Jik was a teenager, and Nora would be in less than another year. Bridie had called her a teenager last night, she remembered with a mixed feeling of pleasure and resentment.

'We want to look up some history stuff,' Jik said. 'Can you tell us where we should look?'

'The reference section is over here,' said the Librarian. She sounded rather annoyed about it. 'Do you need to look up anything in particular? Is it for a school project?'

'Well, just general history,' Jik said.

They followed her across the Library, and found themselves gazing at far too many books for comfort.

'This section is reference only,' said the Librarian. 'That means you can look at the books here, but you can't take them away. The books on these next shelves,' she waved her arm to indicate where she meant, 'can be borrowed, if you have tickets.'

'I have,' Nora said hopefully.

'Right. Be careful with the books, other people will want to read them too.'

The Librarian turned on her heel and stalked back to her desk.

Jik and Nora stared at the shelves of books helplessly.

'Where do we start?' groaned Jik.

It was turning out to be much harder than they had expected.

On Jik's suggestion, they began with the History of Inventions, and looked up Radar. The History was a series of heavy books. They selected the one which covered 'Quin' to 'Red,' and brought it over to the nearest desk, where they could sit and examine it at ease.

'First discovered in the Thirties,' read Jik. 'Developed for use in the Second World War.'

'Well, we knew that,' Nora pointed out. 'I think it would be more useful to look up some history.'

'Right.'

Jik closed the History of Inventions with a bang which drew a frown from the Librarian, and humped it back to the shelf.

There didn't seem to be one particular book which would tell them everything they wanted.

'Dictionary of National Biography,' read out Jik. 'Early Celtic Church History. Irish Pirates of the Middle Ages. The Irish Famine. What do you think?'

'I don't know,' said Nora helpfully.

They stared at the rows of books.

'Maybe we should pick out a few at random, and have a skip through them?' Jik said. 'Here, you take the Church History, and I'll look at this one about pirates.'

'Hey, how mean is that?' protested Nora. 'You get to do the most interesting one.'

But she sat down obediently at the desk and began to leaf through the heavy volume.

'What have you found?' she asked Jik presently. 'This one, at least the bit I'm reading, seems to be mainly about St Patrick.'

'A lot of stuff about Grania, the female pirate who fought with Queen Elizabeth. Quite interesting, actually.'

'So maybe we should start with those two?' Nora said. 'St Patrick would be interesting, I think, and so would Grania.'

'There's about a thousand years between them, plonker,' Jik pointed out. 'And I bet they're both far too early.'

'Well, I'm fed up with this,' Nora said suddenly. 'And we don't even know how to get hold of The Snapper again. And we don't know what happened to Laeg or anything. Let's go home. The best thing would be to ask the Da tonight what he meant by 'the mists of time.''

'Fair enough,' agreed Jik. 'I want to get back in plenty of time to see the hurley match on TV, anyway.'

'Let's go and have a coke first,' Nora suggested. 'There's enough time for that.'

'Sweet. Let's.'

They went into the nearest fast food place, and drank milkshakes, perched on high stools at one of the central tables.

Suddenly Nora stiffened.

Sean O'Reilly was coming through the big glass doors.

She felt her face go red, and carefully kept her eyes away from him.

A moment later his voice sounded in her ear.

'Hi, Nora. Hi, Jik.'

'Hi, Sean,' Jik said. 'How's it goin'?'

'Goin' good.'

'Come and join us when you get served,' Jik suggested.

Nora felt her already red face flame up even more. If this went on she would soon need the fire extinguisher.

'Yeah, right.'

Sean was in the year above Jik at school, but they both played in the school hurley team, at least in the seconds. She hadn't really thought about it before, but, yeah, they were bound to know each other.

In a few minutes Sean came back with a laden tray, and sat down.

'So, Nora,' he said. 'Are you going to hang out at the Computer Club again next term, or what?'

'I should think so. Whatever,' Nora mumbled. Her face seemed to have cooled down, thank goodness. But what could she say? What could she say? Panic mounted.

Then she realised thankfully that Jik was doing all the talking needed, about the forthcoming hurley match.

She studied Sean covertly as he ate.

It hadn't been her imagination.

He could have been Laeg's double.

The lock of fair hair falling into his eyes.

The eyes, bright blue grey with long dark lashes.

His gestures, even, as he waved one hand to explain some point about hurling in his chat with Jik.

Abruptly Nora broke into the conversation.

'Tell me this, Sean. Do you remember a ship called the *White Lady?* Were you ever on it?'

Sean gave her a long, cool look.

'Yeah,' he said. 'Don't you remember? You left in a bit of a hurry, didn't you? But I was okay, as it happened.'

Jik and Nora gaped at him.

## Chapter 14

'Gotta go now,' said Sean.

He stood up in one smooth unhurried movement.

The glass doors swung shut behind him.

Jik and Nora stared at each other.

'Oh.'

# Chapter Fifteen

That night, when Colm had disappeared as usual, and they had watched everything they wanted on the TV, Nora went to bed and wrote up her diary.

*July 18.*

*Wow! We met Sean O'Reilly today, and he sat with us and chatted. I think he liked me? Okay, dream on! But he really did talk to me and Jik more than he's ever done!*

*And when I mentioned the White Lady, he knew what I meant. He talked as if he'd been there. He looks so like Laeg. I don't understand it. How could he be the same person?*

*He seemed angry about something. Does he think we ran out on him?*

*We didn't choose to go. I wish he'd given us a chance to explain. I wish I knew what was going on.*

*I've been thinking about some of the things Laeg and Cuchulain said. It seems that in their day, the women didn't just sit at home and look after the kids, they went out and fought side by side with the men. Great, yeah?*

*I wish I had lived then.*

*But, hey, so what's different?*

*These days, women can do anything they want to, as well, right?*

*Only, somehow, it's hard to believe that, when everyone tells you that girls should get married and stay at home with the babies.*

*Well, okay, Mammy and the Da never said that, but everybody else, like teachers and stuff, say that sort of thing.*

*I want to have a life.*

*I don't want to just do what everyone expects.*

*Bridie Gallagher seems to be able to have it both ways. She has a cool job, but she's grabbed the Da as well.*

*Selfish cow!*

*I wonder if I could get a job programming computers when I leave school? That would be brill!*

*Anyway, why can't they all leave me alone? I don't need grown ups telling me what to do, right?*

*I suppose the Da doesn't really do that. He never bothers about either of us, actually. It would be nice if he did, sometimes.*

*The Da went out as usual tonight. I can't stand that Bridie Gallagher. Trying to put on that she's interested in Jik and me. If she was, she wouldn't take him away every night, nearly.*

*I hoped he was going to stay in. We got him sat down after tea and asked him about the boat, and we were just working round to asking about 'the mists of time', when of course the flipping phone rang. I could have screamed!*

*I think maybe next go we'll try St Patrick's time. It sounded something like!*

*That's if we ever see The Snapper, again, of course?*

*Jik and me are going down to the Marina tomorrow.*

*But if The Snapper isn't there, I'm not sure what we'll do.*


*Later.*

*So Da was out very late again, but anyway he didn't trip down the stairs.*

*I sometimes wonder what he thinks about himself. If it was me, I'd be pretty much ashamed.*

*If we find Peter Lavery and his invention, and bring back some proof, will it make any difference? Will anyone believe us? What kind of proof could we get?*

*If we could find someone who would sign a paper saying Peter invented the thing, the radar, who would we show it to? And how would we explain where we got it?*

*Perhaps we could say we found it in an old box in the attic?*

*Anyway, cross that bridge when we come to it, right?*

*Gonna try, anyhow.*


Nora put her diary away, and crawled into bed.

Tomorrow it would be her turn to choose where they went.

She wondered what it would be like.

Would they have any chance of meeting Sean, or Laeg, again?

And would he be friendly, like in Cuchulain's time?

Or would he still be angry with them?

She turned the light out, and sank down into sleep.

# Chapter Sixteen

The Snapper was reclining peacefully in the stern of the boat, smoking his foul old pipe, when Jik and Nora reached the Marina next day.

Jik was inclined to be indignant.

'He shouldn't get on board our boat without asking, right?' he muttered to Nora as they hurried over.

'Don't be daft! We invited him, didn't we?'

Nora was too pleased to see The Snapper really there again, to worry about whose boat it was.

'Ahoy, shipmates!' greeted The Snapper.

They climbed carefully on board.

'You know how to board a boat properly, I see,' said The Snapper approvingly.

'The Da taught us,' explained Nora. 'Oh, Snapper! It's, like, really brill to see you! I've been so worried about Laeg. What happened after you took us away?'

'Oh, Cuchulain and Laeg between them dealt with that villain well enough,' replied The Snapper coolly. 'They got him tied up, and when the ship reached land they handed him over to the local chief to deal with, before sailing on.'

Nora breathed a sigh of relief. Before she could ask more questions, Jik broke in.

'Are you going to take us somewhere today, Snapper?'

'Well, what do you think?' twinkled The Snapper. 'Do you think you did an unselfish deed last time?'

'Ah, I know Jik did,' said Nora. 'But I'm not sure about me.'

She looked worried.

'You did your unselfish deed right at the start, Nora,' said The Snapper, 'You let Jik have first choice where to go, even though the whole thing was your idea.'

'Oh!' Nora flushed scarlet.

'So, where are we off to today?' asked The Snapper briskly. He stood up and knocked out the ashes of his pipe overboard. 'Any good ideas?'

'It's Nora's turn this time,' said Jik quickly. He hoped that this would mean he had got his unselfish deed over with straight away, like Nora last time.

But The Snapper said nothing except, 'Well, then, Nora?'

Nora hesitated. 'I know we need to go to a much more recent time,' she said slowly. 'We were far too far back last go. But I'm not sure when would be best. I've been reading about St Patrick. It would be cool to go back to his time. And maybe if we happened to meet up with him, he could give us some good advice. Like, he seems to be sorta wise, okay?'

'That's far too long ago,' objected Jik. Then he stopped suddenly, and changed what he had started to say.

'Right, your go, Nora. Whatever.'

'Good lad,' said The Snapper, and Jik couldn't help feeling pleased. 'Early Christian Ireland it is, then. Lots of good mates of mine that you might meet up with there. Let's get this show on the road, so. Got the keys, Jik?'

Jik produced the keys.

The Snapper unlocked the cabin door, and started the engine.

'Do you want to steer, Jik?' he asked. 'Nora might like to get some practice with the ropes. I don't think you need me to steer us out of the Marina, this time.'

Nora wasn't too sure that she did want to help with the ropes and sails. Suppose she had forgotten everything the Da had taught her? Suppose she made a mess of it? Casting off was one thing Helping to put up the sails was quite another.

But Jik said casually, 'Sure, why not? I wouldn't mind a go at steering again.'

Nora found herself back on the pontoon. She cast off the stern rope, ready to step carefully back on board again before it was too late.

'Step, never jump!' the Da had said. 'Try to jump, and slip, you'll be caught between the boat and the pontoon. Be badly hurt. Give yourself plenty of time. Undo the rope smoothly. Step on board straight away.'

Nora took a deep breath, and obeyed the Da's instructions to the letter.

## Chapter 16

Flushed and triumphant, she arrived safely back in the cockpit as the engine began to gain speed. The *Lady Molly* surged forward.

Then it was easy. The Snapper told her exactly what to do. She just had to listen to him. Hand him the right rope at the right moment. Pull hard when he told her to.

Meanwhile Jik was enjoying himself.

He steered the *Lady Molly* carefully between the other boats. He looked for the red port and green starboard markers. He took *Lady Molly* in a safe line down the Marina. It was some time since he had done it, but he didn't make any mistakes. Before long they were out on the open sea again.

The sails were up. The Snapper switched off the engine.

Then The Snapper took the helm as before.

'Hold on tight!' he said.

This time they were expecting the darkness and the roar of the wind, but they still ended up hurled, shaking and speechless, across the cockpit sole.

# Chapter Seventeen

They lay there in a heap while it all happened.

Then Jik, pulling himself together, scrambled up and reached down a hand to pull Nora to her feet.

'Wow!' he said. 'That was something!'

They looked round.

They were on board what seemed to be a much bigger boat than the *White Lady,* where they had met Cuchulain.

Along both sides were seats for oarsmen, mostly unoccupied at present. The middle of the ship was taken up by the wide cockpit sole and the cabin space. The tiller was at a higher level, on a small deck above the stern cabin.

All around, men were working with ropes, loading stores, stowing them away down the hold in the bows of the boat, calling to each other.

There was a smell of sheepskin from the rough jackets the men wore, sweat from their brown, sun-tanned bodies, and spices and olive oil from the galley where food was being prepared for the next meal.

They could see all this at a glance because it was broad daylight.

They huddled together, wondering when someone would notice them.

It didn't take long.

A big man with an air of command leant over one side, speaking to someone in a small rowing boat. A coracle would be the proper name for it, Jik thought. The small boat was drawn up to the side of the bigger vessel.

'We can't take any more this trip,' the big man was saying. 'Yeah, sure, your people have lots of money. Sure, they'll be glad to pay me at the other side, after you've had a free passage – right! I've heard that tale before! We've got quite enough passengers as it is, and I'm taking no more without cash up front. That's final!'

He turned round as he finished speaking, and immediately caught sight of Jik and Nora.

'What!' he roared, 'more stowaways, by Jupiter! Who are you, and how did you get on board my vessel? Barbarians, by your clothes! Have you silver or gold to pay for your voyage? If not, off you go before I set sail!'

Nora quailed before his rough voice and sharp eyes, but Jik spoke out boldly.

'We came aboard while you were speaking to the guy in that boat,' he said. 'We are certainly not stowaways. And, yeah, we have plenty of silver – enough, I guess.'

He pulled a handful of coins out of his jeans pocket. Nora, looking at this, saw that Jik was holding the money the Da had given them yesterday when they came back from the library. Guilt money, because he was about to go out again. There were seven or eight coins, mostly silver. Or silver coloured, at least.

Nora wondered if the ship's captain would know the difference.

Apparently he did not. Seizing the coins Jik held out, he examined them suspiciously.

'H'm. Barbarian coinage. Not worth as much as good Roman money. Still, it'll do,' he added, making up his mind. 'Get on down below decks, then, while we cast off here. I'll show you your sleeping quarters when we're under way. Don't get under my sailors' feet for now.'

He stowed the coins carefully away in a small bag which was secured to his belt, and which he slipped out of sight under his tunic as soon as he had fastened it up again.

As he was doing this, Nora saw, out of the corner of her eye, a movement behind the captain's back. There was a face looking over the rim of the ship.

Then there was a quick flash of colour, and faster than she could have believed, someone hauled himself over the side, dropped silently onto the deck on bare, noiseless feet, and slipped quickly out of sight under a pile of spare sails.

She wondered for a moment if she had imagined it.

But there was no time to wonder more.

The captain was hustling them into the lower cabin, down a long steep ladder.

'And stay there until I tell you you can come up!' he ordered brusquely. 'I can do without passengers getting in my way right now.'

# Chapter 17

Then, turning to the business in hand, he began to hurl orders at his crew, who emerged from various corners of the ship and began to haul on ropes or manipulate oars as he commanded.

'Did you see the stowaway, Jik?' Nora asked excitedly.

'Stowaway?'

'Yeah, he dived up over the side and slid under some stuff while the captain was speaking to us!'

'Hey, why didn't you say?'

'Oh, Jik!' Nora was reproachful. 'And give him away to that awful captain? No way!'

'Yeah, I guess not. Hey, this is cool! I bet we can find him later, and ask him what the game is.'

'And maybe share some of our food with him? If this is a long voyage, they'll have to give us meals.'

'Well, maybe,' Jik said.

He looked round with great interest. They were in a long, low, very dark cabin, with bunks on each side. High above, both to port and to starboard, were two rows of small portholes which let in a meagre light. A rough wooden table took up most of the rest of the space.

'The rowers must be up level with those portholes,' Jik said, thinking aloud. 'Or maybe just above them. This cabin is at the lowest level, I think. It would be for the crew, and maybe for passengers. The captain, and the mate, must have the higher cabin. And I suppose the stores go in the hold we saw, in the bow, for'ard of this.'

'I wonder why the captain talked about 'good Roman coinage?'' Nora said. 'I thought we were in Ireland, not Rome.'

'I thought you read up about it, dafthead,' Jik said. 'St Patrick lived at the time when the Romans occupied England as part of their empire. This must be a Roman merchant ship, trading between England and Ireland.'

'But then we're going the wrong way!' Nora exclaimed. 'We don't want to go to England, we want to stay in Ireland and meet St Patrick, don't we? And you gave him all that money!'

Jik's jaw dropped. 'Hey, right! So now what do we do?'

'We could get off, quick!' Nora offered.

'But as soon as we set foot on land, we go back,' Jik reminded her. 'And, besides, what's that noise I hear?'

It was the rattle of the anchor chain. Seconds later came the smooth splashing of many oars.

The changed motion of the boat told the rest of the story.

They were on their way, travelling across the sea to England, away from Ireland and St Patrick.

They were still staring at each other in dismay, when they heard the sound of feet clattering on the ladder.

A burly looking sailor came slowly into view in the dim light. His feet, clad in heavy seaman's boots, came first.

It was hard to see his face clearly when it finally appeared.

Nora, peering at him through the gloom, felt sure she had seen him before. It was something about the eyes. But she had no time to think about it.

'Captain says passengers can come up now, and he'll show them their quarters,' he announced. 'Look sharp, now! How many of you are there?'

'Well, there's us,' said Jik, coming forward. 'The captain told us to wait down here till he was ready. But I don't know about any others.'

He looked round him dubiously in the half darkness.

'Supposed to be another one, Captain said,' the sailor told him roughly. He peered round the long, low cabin in his turn. 'C'mon, where are you? Out you come!'

A dark shape stood up at the far end of the row of bunks on the starboard side.

Jik and Nora both jumped. They had had no idea than anyone else was in the dark cabin.

'Don't panic, Mister Mariner,' said a voice. 'Here I am.'

Nora stiffened.

Surely she knew that voice?

The other passenger came forward. A little light fell on his face from one of the high portholes.

'Marcus Silvanus, at your service,' he said, sweeping a low bow.

Nora bit her lip to keep from exclaiming aloud.

Fair hair, falling over his face. Grey blue eyes with a touch of irony in their mocking glance.

Were there such things as doubles?

If not, this stranger, calling himself Marcus, was Laeg.

# Chapter Eighteen

There was no time to talk now.

The burly sailor began straight away to bustle the three passengers up the steep ladder to the cockpit.

It was good to be out in the fresh air again.

Jik and Nora were surprised to see how far they had come in such a short time. The land they had left was only a faint green and grey blur in the distance.

All around them, the greeny blue waves sparkled in the occasional sunlight. Gulls still hovered and swooped around the ship, but soon, Nora knew, as land faded out of sight, they would retreat nearer to the shore.

The strong following wind was making the sails billow out, and she noticed that the oarsmen were beginning to relax their efforts. It would be something like turning off the engine once the boat was under way, and letting the sails do the work, she thought. There was no engine on this boat – or rather, ship. They hadn't been invented yet, had they? So the large number of oarsmen took its place.

'Up you go!' said the sailor who had fetched them. He pushed them, none too gently, up a shorter ladder which led to the deck where the tiller was, and to the higher cabin.

The captain was still at the helm, but now he relinquished the tiller to his mate, and turned to his passengers.

'In here!' he said, and showed them the doorway to the cabin above decks.

The three passengers followed him in.

The cabin was much pleasanter than the crews' quarters. It was light and airy by comparison, with windows on each side.

It still seemed primitive to Jik and Nora. There were rough boards along the cabin sides. Thin, folded covers were placed at intervals along their length.

These, they supposed, were the bunks by night and seats by day.

There was little else. Near the doorway on the starboard side Jik noticed a pile of rolled up charts on a low shelf.

Nora was more interested in the small statue on the ledge below the port window. She could not decide if it was a saint or a Roman god, and did not want to show her ignorance by asking.

'Here you are,' said the captain. 'You can pick a bunk each.'

'What about food?' asked Jik. 'When's the next meal?'

'There'll be something along shortly. You'll get what the crew gets, right? We don't cater specially for passengers. This is a merchant ship. Passengers are taken as a favour, and don't you forget it!'

'A favour that fills your purse nicely, I think, Captain Julius,' said Marcus smoothly. 'You would do well to show better manners to this lady. I make no demands for her brother and myself.'

Captain Julius' mouth dropped open.

'Lady? I thought it was a young lad!' he spluttered. 'Why's she dressed like that, then? I don't have any accommodation fit for a lady. I wouldn't have brought her if I'd known. Cause nothing but trouble!'

'The lady has her own reasons for her style of dress, and these are not your business,' was all Marcus would say.

Nora spoke hastily. 'This is fine, really. The voyage isn't too long, I'm sure.'

'We'll be tying up late the day after tomorrow,' Captain Julius acknowledged. 'But I still don't like it. One thing for sure, the crew mustn't know.'

'No problemo,' Jik assured him. 'They won't think of it, any more than yourself, and we won't tell them if you don't.'

The captain grunted. 'Now listen to me!' he said gruffly. 'You won't get no fancy looking after on this ship. Me and my crew have no time for that. You'll have to take care of yourselves. First thing to remember is this. Whenever you move about the ship, keep a firm hold on the guard rails. I don't want any foolishness like passengers slipping over the side.' He glared at them.

'What's more, I don't want to see any of you out on deck if the weather starts to get rough. Stay in your quarters where you ought to be safe enough, you hear me? You can come out for some fresh air if the sea stays calm, but just watch out for squalls.'

Marcus looked at him thoughtfully.

'So, do you expect some bad weather, then, Captain?' he asked.

# Chapter 18

The captain, standing in the doorway of the cabin, looked anxiously up at the sky. He seemed to be more worried than he wanted to show.

Then he licked one finger and held it up to the wind.

'Freshening,' he said at last, speaking more to himself than to them.

'Ah, who knows?' he said finally. 'There's some signs of rough weather blowing up – but maybe it'll come to nothing. We'll be calm enough for a while yet anyway. But pay heed to me and don't be running any silly risks, the lot of you!'

They nodded. Jik and Nora were well aware that people who took silly risks at sea, as the Da had often said, deserved anything they got.

'It'll be calm enough tonight, I reckon,' the captain concluded. 'So, into the cabin with you, and your supper'll be here shortly. Then you can settle down for the night.'

Grumbling, Captain Julius made his way back to the helm.

Jik and Nora were left alone with the so-called Marcus.

But before there was time to speak, a shadow on the cabin door announced the arrival of supper.

The same burly sailor came in abruptly and set a full tray on the ledge by the entrance, pushing aside the rolled charts.

'Here – help yourselves,' he said. 'Captain'll be along in a few minutes for his share.'

Jik and Nora looked round for somewhere to sit.

Marcus collected some bread and a chunk of hot, spiced meat from the tray, along with a cup of water from the jug, and went to lie along the nearest bunk.

Jik and Nora followed his example.

To their annoyance, Captain Julius came back almost at once, before the sailor had left.

Seizing what seemed like much more than his fair share of the bread and meat, he threw himself down in a reclining position on one of the bunks.

It was clear that there would be no opportunity to talk privately until morning.

Jik, Nora and Marcus, seeing that darkness had begun to descend rapidly, settled themselves for sleep.

It was some time before Nora was able to get over.

For some reason, although she could see nothing, she felt sure that a pair of eyes, peering round the doorway of the cabin, was fastened on them.

Eyes fastened mostly, she felt, on Marcus.
Was someone about to attack him, as Laeg had been attacked?
But nothing happened, and finally she drifted off.

# Chapter Nineteen

Nora was wakened by the bright sun tickling her eyelids.

It was morning, and the captain had gone. Back up to take his turn on the helm, she thought.

Slipping out of her bunk, Nora wandered off to find the heads. They were primitive enough, but better than nothing. Then she came back to the cabin to find both boys stretching and ready to follow her example.

On the ledge where supper had been placed last night, was more bread and water, with some strong smelling cheese.

The fresh sea air had made Nora extra hungry. By the time the boys came back, she was well into her second chunk of bread, and had found that the cheese, though sharp and strong, was definitely edible.

'I hope the captain has had his share!' grinned Jik, starting in busily. 'Because I don't plan to leave him too much!'

For a few minutes there was nothing to be heard but the sound of munching.

Then, almost at the same moment, it dawned upon Jik and Nora that this was their opportunity to find out the truth about Marcus.

Nora spoke first.

'It is you, Laeg, isn't it?' she said in a rush. 'Or Sean? Ah, who are you? How did you get here? And are you the stowaway I saw getting over the side?'

The boy stared at her in amazement.

'Stowaway?' he asked. 'I paid for my passage like yourselves.'

'Never mind about that now!' interrupted Jik impatiently. 'We want to know which you are, Laeg or Sean or Marcus, and why that guy we rescued was attacking you, and how on earth you keep managing to turn up in the middle of our adventures!'

'Well, I might ask you that,' said the boy. 'But maybe I know more about you than you do about me. It's simple, right?'

Suddenly he broke off. There was the sound of feet approaching the cabin door.

The door opened. A head appeared round it, followed by a spry, cheerful sailor. He looked, Nora thought, far more friendly than anyone else they had met so far on this ship.

'Greetings, shipmates,' he said. 'Sorry to interrupt. I'm Flavius Maximus, the mate of this fine merchant ship, the *Seahorse*. They call me Maximus as a bit of a joke, me not being all that tall, or broad either. But good things come in small packages, I say.'

Jik, Nora, and Marcus hastily returned his friendly greeting.

'My turn for the helm tonight,' Flavius explained. 'So I get to take a turn in the bunk for now. Captain plans to sleep at night, while poor old Flavius steers. And since he's captain, that's how it goes. So if you don't mind, I'll ask you people to either sit quietly, or take yourselves elsewhere, till I get me a bit of shut-eye, right?'

'Right,' said Jik hastily. 'C'mon, you guys, let's head out.'

They made their way out past the helm, past the scowling Captain Julius, and along the port deck to the bow.

There was no one else within earshot.

They leaned on the rail, gazing down at the swift waves rushing past the stem of the boat. Overhead, the sky seemed full of rushing clouds.

'Okay,' said Jik. He turned his head to look Marcus firmly in the eye. 'Right, man. Tell.'

'There's nothing much to tell,' said the boy slowly.

'Well, start with why that seaman was attacking you,' Jik ordered brusquely.

'It was my knife, this knife that I wear in my belt, okay? He was after it.'

He pulled out the knife and showed it to them.

Seeing it close to for the first time, Jik and Nora both noticed the strange inscriptions on the hilt, the gleaming sharpness of the blade. They gaped at Marcus.

'But why?' Nora managed eventually.

'It came to me from my Dad. He picked it up on holiday abroad one year, in the Basque country. And the seller told him it was incredibly old, belonged to the Druids, to some wonder worker called Bantha, he said. Should never be used for anything ordinary, or it would bring a curse on the user. Dad thought it was just a joke, but I'm not so sure.'

He paused and his face grew grim.

# Chapter 19

'Mum and Dad were killed in a car crash last year. The knife came to me, then. But I've wondered. Had the knife anything to do with their accident? Dad had been using it to lever off the wheel trim when he had to change the wheel in an emergency, and couldn't find his screw driver.' He looked at them, then turned his face away. 'I felt I had to know if there was any truth in the story. So – you know your friend The Snapper?'

They nodded.

'Well, I've known him for quite a long time, now. And he's been taking me back in time, to track down the history of the knife, if I can. That's all. I don't know who that man was, or what he knew about the knife, but he must have seen me use it, and he was certainly trying to take it away from me. But Cuchulain helped me throw him off.'

'We would have helped, too!' Nora burst out. 'But The Snapper took us away. We couldn't stop him!'

Marcus smiled.

'So that was it?' he said. 'I couldn't help wondering. Sorry.'

'That's all right.' Jik spoke coldly. He didn't like being thought a coward.

It was left to Nora to say, 'But who are you, really?'

'I'm whoever I choose to be,' he said. 'Right now, I'm Marcus.'

They looked at him suspiciously. The explanation didn't seem to explain anything.

Suddenly Jik's eye was distracted by a movement behind the pile of boxes beside him – stores still waiting to be lowered into the nearby hold.

Catching Nora's eye, he made a sign of zipping up his mouth. Then he did the same with Marcus.

Speaking casually, he moved along the rail.

'Looks like the waves are getting bigger. Hope there's not a storm coming up.'

By now he was right beside the boxes.

With a sudden pounce he lunged behind the nearest one and his hand shot out.

There was a shout and the noise of boxes falling over.

A second later, Jik emerged from the wreckage holding some-one's arms firmly in both hands.

'Gottcha!'

The captive wriggled wildly, panting. But by now Marcus had grasped him from behind, and his position was hopeless.

Nora stood, her hands to her mouth, staring thunderstruck. Suddenly she let out an exclamation.

'Jik! It's the stowaway!'

They all three stared at what they had caught.

It was a boy of about Marcus' age, or a few years older. He was very thin and had a wild mop of hair which fell over his dirty face. He was dressed in a ragged tunic and britches, with a dirty sheepskin slung round his shoulders, rather like the ship's crew, and like them his skin was brown and weather-beaten, as if he had spent most of his time outdoors. But unlike them, he looked frightened and half-starved.

'Let me go!' he said. 'What harm have I done to you?'

'Let him go, Jik!' said Nora at once. 'He's right, he hasn't done us any harm. Only taken a free passage from that awful captain. And he said he would pay for it on the other side!'

'Not so fast, Nora,' Marcus said quietly. 'I think we need to know a bit more about this lad before we let him loose to roam the ship.'

Jik nodded. 'Right. Hey, you, tell us a bit more, then. Who are you, for a start?'

'It depends.' said the boy sulkily. 'I've been called lots of things.'

'I'll bet!' whispered Jik to Nora, grinning.

'I suppose my proper name was Maewyn. That was what my own family called me, I mean.'

'So, where are your own family, then?' asked Nora with interest. 'And why aren't you with them?'

'I was captured, that's why. Don't know where my folks are – back home in Britain, I guess.'

Nora's mouth formed a silent, 'Wow!'

'Oh, please do tell us your story properly!' she exclaimed. 'It sounds, like, wild!'

'Let's sit down,' suggested Marcus, 'and let Maewyn tell us his story in peace.'

'Okay,' agreed Jik. 'But let's keep a good lookout in case anyone comes. If they catch Maewyn, he's in big trouble, right?'

They sat in a semi-circle, and the boy began.

# Chapter Twenty

'It was quite a long time ago – I was only a kid,' Maewyn said. 'I was living at home with my parents in West Britain. It was a smallish village. My father was the Christian priest. But I have to say I didn't pay a lot of attention to what he said then. Like, it seemed to me a waste of time.

'Then one day a horde of barbarians from Ireland raided our village and took lots of us captive. It was terrible!' Maewyn shivered at the memory.

'They took us over the sea to Ireland, and sold most of us as slaves. I suppose I was lucky, in a way. My best mate, Kieran, was sort of good-looking, I guess, and he was sold to a well-off chief as a 'personal servant'. We all knew what that meant, of course.'

'What?' Nora asked innocently.

Maewyn laughed bitterly. He said briefly. 'A lover – maybe permanently, if the chief decided to keep him. Or sold on, if he got sick of him. Kieran, of all people!'

The others were silent.

After a short pause, Maewyn went on.

'As I said, you could say I was sort of lucky. I was bought by a farmer, and taken north to his land round Slemish, and he put me to work looking after his sheep. I had food and clothes, sorta way, but I have to say there were nights when I almost froze to death.

'I missed my family and friends something fierce, too.

'And, it was funny, but being out at night with the sheep, looking up at the stars, I got to feeling that some of the stuff my father used to go on about maybe wasn't such rubbish as I used to think. Like, maybe there was someone up there.

'Anyway, one night I heard a voice in my head, and it said, 'Time to go home, son. Your ship's ready and waiting.'

'I knew I'd better go, or spend the rest of my life as a slave in Ireland.

'Same time, I had an idea, just like, a sorta idea, that some day it would be right for me to come back. Help the people who took me captive.

'But I wasn't ready to think about that just yet. No way!

'So I got some stuff together. Next evening I made off. Under cover of darkness.

'I didn't know anywhere near Slemish where I could get a ship – it's quite far inland – so I planned to trek back down to where the ship brought me in all those years ago.

'I knew where the farmer kept his money pouch, and I managed to take some coins out of that, and some bread and meat from the kitchen, before I left. The guard dogs didn't bark and give me away, naturally. They all knew me.

'I thought I should be okay – that I had everything I needed.

'But it's been a long journey, best part of a hundred miles, maybe.

'The food ran out quite soon. At first I bought some, with the money I'd taken, although I'd been hoping to keep that for my passage on the ship.

'Then the money came to an end, too. My last coin was taken from me by force, by a couple of wandering outlaws. They jumped me one evening, in the woods. Like, leapt out from the bushes and grabbed me.

'They were both bigger than me, and there were two of them, right?

'Not a lot I could do.

'I suppose they hoped to get more.

'When they saw how little I had, they beat me up. Out of spite, I guess.

'They left me to die or recover, or whatever, they didn't care which.

'Okay, so I got over it and went on.

'After that I had to wait my chance and hang round a village at night-time, every few days. When it got dark I would manage to slip into one of the huts while they were sleeping, and eat whatever I could find. Take some food with me as well, if there was any to spare.'

'Eat in and take-away,' murmured Jik, mostly to himself.

'One night the man of the house woke up, and chased me. He caught me and gave me such a hammering, but his wife was kind, and made him stop, and bandaged my cuts and gave me some bread and cheese. She reminded me of my mother.'

Maewyn stopped for a moment to wipe the back of one hand across his eyes. They all looked away hastily.

'Then I got to the coast, near where the ship landed when they brought me to Ireland. I didn't want to run into the same slave traders, right, but I thought if I was careful I could dodge them, and I could get some sort of merchant ship – something a bit more legit. When I saw this one, I just knew, somehow, that it was the one for me.

'But then the captain wouldn't let me on board. I knew I had to manage somehow. I'd offered him money. But he wanted to see it up front, so that was no good. I told him my family would pay him on the other side, but he wouldn't believe me.

'I knew this was the ship that I'd been told was ready for me. So I scrambled on when he wasn't looking.

'Since then I've been dodging about, hiding.'

He paused, and looked at his three listeners.

'If you guys will help me, it might still work out.'

'Of course we'll help you!' Nora said eagerly. 'Won't we?'

She looked at both Jik and Marcus.

'Yeah, right,' said Jik. 'Sure thing.'

Marcus nodded agreement.

A sudden look of suspicion came into the boy's eyes. 'Hey, don't get me wrong. I don't have anything to offer in return, here! So don't think you're going to get anything back, right?'

'Maewyn,' said Marcus, 'we know you've had a rough time, man. But, like, you either trust us or you don't. All we can say is that we aren't in this for anything we can get out of it. We're not gonna get mad about what you just said. But, hey, maybe you might apologise?'

'Yeah, right, sorry,' muttered the boy.'But some of the guys I've met –'

Jik decided to change the subject. 'What age are you, anyway, Maewyn?' he asked.

'Well, I was in my mid teens when they took me,' Maewyn said. 'I guess I'm around nineteen or twenty by now. You lose track, out in the hills.'

Nora, who hadn't really been listening to some of the recent conversation, broke in.

'Shouldn't we be looking for somewhere to hide Maewyn instead of sitting round gassing?' she said. 'If we aren't careful someone will turn up and catch him.'

No sooner were the words out of her mouth, than they heard, getting louder and louder as they approached, the sound of heavy seaman's boots on the deck behind them.

'Quick, Maewyn, get back behind the boxes,' whispered Jik. 'We'll stall him, whoever it is!'

It was the rough, burly sailor who had come to take them to the captain yesterday.

He glared at them bad-temperedly.

'This is no place for passengers,' he said. 'Captain told you there was a storm coming up soon. Get back to your quarters and stay there, where you won't be blown overboard.'

'Why does everyone on this ship have to be so rude?' muttered Jik to Nora.

'Except the mate – he was all right,' Nora whispered back.

'We came out from our cabin for a very good reason,' Marcus was answering the sailor. 'Your Mate, Flavius, was trying to sleep. We came away so as not to disturb him.'

'Well, tough for Flavius,' growled the sailor. 'Captain's orders. You're to get back, before the storm comes. He reckons it's pretty near by now. Why can't you just sit quietly on your bunks? And if Flavius don't like it, he can lump it.'

'Okay.' Marcus shrugged, and began to turn away towards the stern of the ship. Jik and Nora started to follow him.

Nora was wondering miserably what would happen to Maewyn when the storm broke. At the very least, he was bound to get completely soaked.

The ship gave a sudden lurch, as an unusually high, hard wave crashed against the bows. They all, the sailor included, found themselves staggering and grabbing for safety at the rail beside them.

But that was not all.

As the ship tilted sharply in the sudden squall, the pile of boxes fell awkwardly across the deck, rolling dangerously about their feet.

In the space behind them, crouched down as small as he could make himself, Maewyn squatted, clearly exposed to the sailor's view.

With an angry roar, the burly sailor pounced on Maewyn, and dragged him out into the open.

# Chapter 20

One of Maewyn's feet was caught in the tangle of ropes. He twisted in vain to escape from the sailor's grasp.

Marcus, almost without thought, it seemed to Nora, seized the dagger from his belt and slashed wildly at the rope.

A moment's work and Maewyn was free, and scrambling to his feet. He fled along the deck, dodging round the sailor.

The sailor's hand shot out to stop him.

But before he could catch hold of the boy, Marcus' foot shot out and the sailor, tripping over it, went sprawling.

Jik and Nora clung to the sailor's tunic, trying to prevent him struggling to his feet.

Marcus called after the fleeing boy.

'Maewyn! Stop! You'll run straight into the captain on the helm!'

But Maewyn either didn't hear or was too panic-stricken to heed the warning.

Straight as an arrow he sped along, head down to watch his feet, blind to what lay ahead.

It was just as Marcus had foreseen.

The captain heard the sound of running feet. Handing the tiller to the nearest crewman, he stepped out from the helm right into Maewyn's path.

Straight into him ran Maewyn, his head taking the captain full in the stomach, knocking the breath out of the big man.

But not badly enough to disable him.

The captain's right hand shot out.

A moment later Maewyn hung struggling and helpless in the grasp of one huge hand.

The captain shook him vehemently. Then, regaining his breath, he roared,

'By Jupiter, what have we here?'

Jik, Nora and Marcus arrived panting.

'He's a friend of ours, Captain!' Nora gasped urgently. 'Let him go! We'll pay for his passage!'

But the captain was too angry to listen.

'Stowaway on my ship, would you?' he roared. 'I'll teach you, you rascally thief!'

One hand still grasped Maewyn by the neck, the other drew back and formed itself into a fist.

Nora cried out.

But the blow never fell.

Just at that moment, the storm broke.

# Chapter Twenty One

All those on their feet found themselves staggering helplessly, falling, reaching desperately for the nearest rail or woodwork to grasp hold of.

The captain, knocked sideways by the rush of the waves against the ships' sides, and almost blinded by the thick gusts of rain, let go of Maewyn without even thinking about it. His only concern was to get back to the helm of his ship and battle with all his skill against the elements.

It was suddenly dark. A fierce wind whistled around their ears.

Maewyn, dropped to the deck like a rag doll, rolled helplessly about their feet.

The captain forced his way back to the tiller. In the flashes of lightening, Nora saw that his face was grim and desperate.

They clung with both hands to whatever was near, aware that if they let go, they would be at the mercy of the storm.

It was useless, now, to think of trying to get to the cabin. The risk was too great.

All they could do was hang grimly on until the storm blew itself out.

The burly sailor had managed to scramble to his feet again.

Unnoticed by Nora, Jik or Marcus, he staggered after them, arrived at Marcus' side.

His fist caught Marcus a blow on the side of his head, a blow heavy enough to send Marcus flying to the deck.

The tilting ship sent him sliding to the edge, just where there was a gap in the bulwark, but the sailor, jumping after him, was able to prevent Marcus from going overboard. His strong arms and hands gripped Marcus and held him back from disaster. It seemed that although he had attacked Marcus, he didn't want him to disappear into the depths of the sea. What was going on? Nora leapt forward. We have to rescue Marcus, she thought. This can't be allowed to happen! Then she saw that the burly sailor was trying to wrestle the dagger from Marcus' hands.

It was like a horrible rewind of the attack on Laeg aboard Cuchulain's ship, the *White Lady*.

Through Nora's head went the thought, 'What was The Snapper doing to let us in for this? Oh, if only he would come and rescue us!'

She looked round for Maewyn, but could not see where he had rolled to.

Then came another huge flash of lightening.

The ship rolled even more fiercely. The sailor grappling with Marcus began to shriek. Jik and Nora hurled themselves upon him, desperate to stop whatever he was doing. Marcus threshed about desperately, trying to squirm out of the sailor's grasp. Just at the same moment the ship gave an enormous heave. The burly sailor began to slide across the deck. His grip on Marcus had loosened under the assault of Jik and Nora, but he still had hold of him by one foot. Jik tried hopelessly to grab the sailor by the nearest arm, but it was too late. Before they could stop him, he had plunged off the deck, taking Marcus with him.

Jik, panting fiercely, caught Marcus by his tunic and one arm. Nora, unable to stop herself screaming, seized hold of Jik round the waist. She looked round wildly for something to cling to, and found that she could grasp the bulwark with one hand.

The waves still rolled the ship roughly backwards and forwards.

'Hang on!' Jik ground out desperately through his teeth.

Nora and Jik were pulling fiercely at Marcus, trying to move him back over the edge of the deck. It seemed impossible. Marcus, trying to help, kicked and lunged wildly.

Then, unbelievably, they felt the weight disappear, and all three of them shot backwards across the deck in a tumbled heap.

'What happened?' gasped Jik.

'My boot!' Marcus half sobbed, half shouted. 'It's gone! The boot slipped from my foot!'

The burly sailor, his support vanishing, disappeared beneath the fierce waves.

The horrified watchers could only cling helplessly to the rails, trying desperately to prevent themselves following the sailor overboard.

It was then that Nora saw Maewyn.

Lit up suddenly by a flash of lightning, his face seemed strangely high up.

Then she realised why.

## Chapter 21

Maewyn was climbing the rigging.

At that same moment, it seemed that everyone had noticed him.

'Come down, you fool!' roared the captain, even his great voice almost carried away by the howling wind and crashing waves. 'You'll be swept off and killed!'

But Maewyn continued to climb.

Then it seemed that he had reached up as high as he wanted to go.

All eyes were fixed on him as he clung by arms and legs to the rigging, high above the deck.

He must, Nora thought, be able to see the whole little ship, and the fierce, lashing seas around it.

Then Maewyn lifted his right arm and stretched it out in a commanding gesture. He shouted, and his voice was louder than the captain's.

'In the name of the Lord God, High King over Heaven and Earth, I command you, storm, to cease! I command you, waters, to be calm!'

The noise stopped as if someone had turned off a switch.

Nora gasped.

Daylight was returning.

All around them, the waters lay still and peaceful.


For a moment no one spoke.

Then Maewyn, both hands again on the rigging, scrambled swiftly down.

As his feet touched the deck, the captain surged forward.

But a very different captain from the angry bully who had seized Maewyn only minutes earlier.

Falling on his knees before the boy, he caught hold of Maewyn's hand and began to kiss it, weeping hysterically.

'Thank you, thank you, whoever you are! A worker of miracles! My ship is at your service! Forgive me for not recognising your power before! What can I do to make it up to you?'

'You could get him into the cabin and give him some dry clothes, and some food, before he catches his death of cold!' said Nora tartly.

'Yeah, that would be it,' agreed Maewyn meekly. He seemed dazed, as if he was as much surprised by his actions as the rest of them.

'And us, too,' added Jik smartly.

They herded up to the cabin, and the captain, falling over himself in a mixture of gratitude and fear, to do as the strange boy wanted, sent crew members scurrying for food, and himself produced clean, dry tunics from his own spare equipment.

Presently they were lying, dry and wrapped in warm woolly clothes, on the bunks of the upper cabin, munching bread and cold left-over meat, and sipping warmed up mead.

To Jik's amusement, the Mate, Flavius, was sleeping peacefully on one of the far bunks where they had left him, and seemed to have been oblivious to both the storm and the excitement.

Grinning, Jik pointed him out to the others.

'A wise man,' commentated Marcus. 'It's not really nighttime yet, but it certainly feels like it. It's been a long day. Why don't we follow his example?'

Not many minutes later, the cabin was silent except for the occasional small snores of Flavius Maximus.

Jik, Nora, Marcus and Maewyn were fast asleep.

# Chapter Twenty Two

It was morning by the time any of them woke.

Staggering to her feet, Nora went looking for the heads, and after that, for any sign of breakfast.

Flavius was at the helm. At some stage, Captain Julius had taken his place on one of the bunks.

'Hey, how about some breakfast, Flavius?' Nora asked pleasantly.

'Certainly, lad!' answered the mate. 'You're a bit later than the crew this morning, see, but we can fix you up with something.'

Raising his voice, he called for one of the crew, and before long Nora and the others were eating bread and meat again.

None of them were quite sure what to say to Maewyn about last night. Had he really calmed the storm?

What had actually happened?

Maewyn himself seemed reluctant to talk about it. He seemed, Nora thought, as surprised as any of them.

By tacit consent, they left the subject alone, and concentrated on eating.

'This food's okay, and plenty of it,' said Jik. 'But there isn't much variety, is there?'

'Well, considering that at home you live on peanut butter sandwiches, you're a fine one to be talking about variety!' exclaimed Nora.

'That's what I mean – lots of bread, but no peanut butter!' explained Jik.

Breakfast over, Nora said, 'Jik, you and I need to talk to some of the crew – don't we? Flavius, the mate, for starters, right?'

'Well, if you think there's any point,' shrugged Jik.

'This is about your family invention, yeah?' Marcus said, while Maewyn looked puzzled.

'You've got it,' acknowledged Jik.

'Well, Flavius is up at the helm right now, so how about it?' Nora persisted.

They trooped out.

It was a beautiful morning. The sun glinted on the rippling water. A fresh, following wind billowed out the sails, but there was no sign of the wild gusts of the previous evening.

Flavius was standing at the helm, one hand casually on the tiller, the other holding a chunk of bread which he tore at with his teeth from time to time.

As they approached, he looked round, grinned, and winked at them.

'Well, shipmates!' he said. 'And how are you this fine morning? Sleep well?'

Nora looked determined.

It had been her suggestion to come back to St. Patrick's time. She felt responsible. It was up to her to get any information that might be available.

'We want to talk to you, Flavius,' she began.

'Fine by me,' said the mate cheerfully. 'But if you hold on for a minute, Captain Julius should be coming to relieve me, and we might have a short chat before I go to catch up on my beauty sleep.'

Nora agreed eagerly.

'We'll go and wait over by the bows,' she suggested. The others nodded agreement. No one was particularly keen to meet Captain Julius again, changed man or not.

They were just in time.

They reached the bows, leant over against the bulwarks. They could hear the roar of the captain's voice approaching from the stern.

They stood gazing into the murky depths, trying to spot fish or seaweed, but unable to see more than a few feet below the surface.

A moment later, a voice spoke softly behind them.

It was Flavius.

'Well, then, shipmates. Don't be keeping me from my bunk longer than you can help. What did you want to ask me?'

Nora took a deep breath.

'It's about how you steer the ship,' she began. 'We wondered what your system is?'

'Why, I steer by the sun by day and the moon and stars by night, my dear,' replied Flavius merrily. 'What did you think I did?'

'Oh.'

Nora could not help the disappointment showing in her voice.

# Chapter 22

'It'll be a long time yet before even the compass comes into general use,' went on Flavius. 'And as for the little invention you and your brother are interested in – the predecessor to radar –!'

Jik interrupted.

'Wait a minute! How do you know anything about that?'

Flavius chuckled.

'Well, how do you think?'

Nora stared at him slowly. As she looked, Flavius winked at her again.

'Snapper!' she exclaimed. 'It is you, isn't it? What on earth are you doing here?'

Flavius grinned. From the depths of his tunic he pulled out an old white cap, and put it on his head.

There was no doubt about it. He was The Snapper.

'I thought you might need a little help, this time,' The Snapper explained. 'As well as my good friend Marcus, that is. You remember I told you I have lots of friends in this time? Old Flavius was happy to take a little holiday in our century, and let me take his place for a couple of days. I'm surprised you didn't recognise me sooner! But it's a good disguise, I reckon!'

# Chapter Twenty Three

They stared at him. His face was stained brown, his hair, instead of white, was dark, and clipped short, and he was clean-shaven. Except for the eyes, bright and twinkling, he was so different that they could not blame themselves for failing to recognise him.

'Well, my hearties,' The Snapper said, 'have you been enjoying yourselves?'

'It's been great, okay,' Jik acknowledged. 'But –' He paused.

'But it hasn't got you any further on your search, right?' said The Snapper.

'No,' agreed Nora sadly. 'We've come too far back again. Jik was right.'

'Of course,' Jik put in half jokingly.

'But I really thought, like, if we met St. Patrick we could get his advice,' Nora went on. 'He must be pretty wise. And the worst of it is, we haven't even seen him! We're in completely the wrong place.'

'Is that so?' The Snapper was grinning.

'What do you mean?' asked Nora in surprise.

'You haven't met St. Patrick, you say, Nora?' The Snapper asked. 'I thought you'd read up his story? Use the head, girl!'

Nora stared at him.

It was Jik who burst out, 'You don't mean –?'

Nora looked at them. Both Jik and The Snapper were gazing at Maewyn.

Everyone seemed to understand something, except Nora. Apart from Marcus, who was gazing into the distance, saying nothing.

Maewyn stared back at them in a puzzlement at least equal to Nora's.

'Let me introduce you to the man himself,' said The Snapper. 'Maewyn of Wales, later known as Patrick because he came from what the Romans called the Patrician families. We would say the upper crust – the nobs.'

'But – but –' Nora stammered. 'He's just a boy. St Patrick should be an old man with a beard! And how can he be a saint, when he goes around stealing and lying and so on? Oh. I'm sorry, Maewyn, I know you felt you had to do those things to survive. But I don't understand!'

'We all have to start somewhere, Nora,' said The Snapper gently. 'And we all make mistakes when we're young.'

He grinned at Maewyn.

'The lad has a lot to learn yet. But you saw him calming the storm. Didn't that make you think?'

'I suppose it should have.' Nora admitted. 'And I suppose his story should have made me recognise him too.'

'Too right it should,' Jik agreed.

'But that means he can't tell us anything helpful, either?' Nora said.

'All the same,' Jik told her, 'It's been really something, meeting St Patrick himself.'

'Yep, it has,' Nora said eagerly. 'I'll never think of saints as old and boring again. Maewyn, it's been ace seeing what you're really like!'

'I don't understand,' said Maewyn in his turn.

'Never mind, lad,' said The Snapper. 'You'll understand all in good time.'

It was then that Nora suddenly noticed the expression on Marcus' face.

'What is it?' she asked softly.

'Well. ' He hesitated. 'It's just.' Then abruptly he burst out. 'It's that sailor. 'Okay, he tried to steal my knife, but I can't help thinking that if I hadn't been kicking out so hard, maybe we could have dragged him back on board. My boot probably wouldn't have come off, see? And it was my fault, then, that he was left to drown in that awful ocean.'

'No, he wasn't,' said Maewyn briskly. 'Don't forget the sea was calm only minutes after he went into it. I saw him myself, while I was still high enough up to see all round, swimming away from the ship quite strongly. No need to blame yourself!'

'But will he have been able to keep swimming for long enough to reach any land?' asked Marcus doubtfully.

'He didn't need to,' said The Snapper. 'He'll just have gone back to his own time.'

# Chapter 23

'What, was he time-travelling, too?' exclaimed Nora.

'Certainly!' said The Snapper. 'Why should you, and Marcus here, be the only ones?'

'So,' said Nora slowly. 'I was right in thinking he looked familiar? It was the same man who tried to steal the dagger in Cuchulain's time?'

'That's right,' said The Snapper. 'He's a Druid. A priest. To him, the dagger is of the utmost importance.'

'But why?' asked Marcus. He drew the dagger carefully from its place in his belt.

'A druid priest?' Maewyn interrupted. 'And this is a druid dagger?' He reached over to take it from Marcus' hand. 'Oh, then I can tell you a bit about it. This looks like one of the daggers they use for sacrifice. See the inscription on the hilt? It's a bit worn, but it says it belongs to someone called Bantha, and there's a bit about it being sacred to the service of the spirits, if I'm reading it right. It counts as sacred to any druid, and the sight of it being used casually by someone else for all sorts of ordinary things would be awful, I should think. There are still lots of Druids back where I live, in Wales, in spite of the coming of Christianity some time back. I've seen more than I want to of their religion.' He shuddered. 'My mate Kieran and I sneaked into one of their ceremonies once, just to watch, and I've wished ever afterwards that we hadn't. Human sacrifice, see?'

'And you mean this knife would have been used for that?' asked Nora, her eyes like saucers. She reached out to touch the hilt, and gave a queer little shudder.

'Yeah. So now you know what you're up against.' Maewyn looked seriously at Marcus. He handed back the dagger, and Marcus took it almost reluctantly.

'What I don't understand, Snapper,' Nora said slowly. She had been thinking. 'What I don't understand is how a person like that priest gets to time travel. Surely he hasn't been doing unselfish deeds each time?'

'Good point, young Nora,' said Snapper jovially. 'But I didn't say he travelled with me, or any of our people, did I? There's an opposition party, right? And they arrange their time travel on quite another basis. Good deeds don't come into it, not by a long way! That's who this priest travels with.'

'An opposition party?' Jik said.

'Yeah, you've heard of good and evil, right? Our side is working for good. But there's another side, and you may say they're working for evil, see?'

'Gosh!' said Jik. Nobody else said anything for a moment. Then,

'Meanwhile, shipmates, any minute now we'll be seeing land in sight. Better say goodbye to Maewyn and get ready for the transfer back!' The Snapper's voice broke in on their thoughts.

'But we can't leave it there!' Nora said. 'Suppose this priest follows Marcus, I mean Sean, back to our own times! We need to get together when we're home!'

'I don't see why not,' said the so-called Marcus. For the first time he sounded less friendly, more like the Sean O'Reilly of their own time. 'It's really up to you two, isn't it? If you really want to see me, you know where I live!'

There was no time for more.

From the rigging, a voice called, 'Land ahoy!'

Then suddenly it was dark, and they were being thrown sideways about the boat.

A moment later, they were sprawling on the deck of the *Lady Molly*.

# Chapter Twenty Four

*July 20*
*Today we reckoned we needed to do two things.*
*Talk to Sean.*
*Find out more from the Da.*
*Sean seemed a bit upset, or ratty, maybe, that we hadn't recognised him at first for sure, and didn't seem clear about meeting him in Cuchulain's time. I don't want him to think we've just not bothered again.*


*Later.*
*Turned out that Sean wasn't at home.*
*We trekked all the way over to his uncle's house. Jik said he knew where it was.*
*But when we got there, nobody would answer the door at first, and we were just giving up when the door opened a couple of inches and a fat woman poked her head out. She had the sucker part of a vacuum cleaner in one hand.*
*'Well?' she said. She sounded v. irritated. 'There's no one in but me, and I'm just the cleaner. So you'd better come back some other time.'*
*So we had to come away again.*
*V. disappointing.*
*It's quite a big house, with an ace garden.*
*Jik says that since Sean's Ma and Da were killed in that car crash a year ago, he lives with his uncle who has something to do with stocks and shares.*
*So then, when we got home, we reckoned we'd better see what the Da says about the invention, if we can get him settled down to talk.*

*Later.*

*I opened a tin of beans and sausages for tea, and Jik nipped out to the chippie and got chips for us all, and Da seemed pleased that we'd bothered.*

*We sat round the kitchen table and ate, and we got the Da talking, all right.*

*He wanted to start with some of his adventures when he was a sailor, and we just let him ramble on for a while.*

*Mind you, it was interesting enough.*

*Only we wanted to know about the pre-radar thingy.*

*So, right, we got him round to that at last, and we asked him about Faraday, who was a friend of Peter Lavery.*

*'Faraday was a great man,' the Da said. 'The inventor of electricity, you see. That was what put the idea into Peter's head. Peter was a bit of a scientist himself, of course, or he couldn't have thought of it. Something about reflecting sound waves. Or radio waves, was it? I'm a bit vague about the details, right? I'm no scientist myself. But old Peter was years ahead of his time.*

*'Only he never got the patent organised, okay? He did some trials on the Nancy Belle, I think, and it was all going right. But then his father died, and he gave up sailing to take over the family business – much like myself, lads –'*

*'Oh, yeah?' I thought. 'And you work really hard at it, right? Go there once every few months, whether you need to or not!'*

*Jik made a face at me, so he was thinking the same thing –*

*'– and he got so bogged down in the business that he didn't make any move about the patent until years later. And, sad to say, he died of a heart attack before he got it finalised.*

*'I often think what a shame it was that my great granda didn't follow up on it. But there, maybe he didn't have the right information to hand, and wouldn't have known where to start. And the same goes for my Da and myself.'*

*Jik was keeping nudging me all this time, and at last he burst out, 'Da, when did all this happen? Which century, I mean?'*

*It was the right question, sure, but the Da wasn't best pleased at being interrupted in his best story.*

*'I'd ha' thought, Jik my lad,' he said sharply, 'you'd have no problem working that out for yourself? Which century did Faraday live in, eh?'*

*We hadn't a clue.*

# Chapter 24

*'Look it up, boy! Look it up!' was all the Da would say.*

*It was pretty sickening.*

*He thought Jik didn't really believe him, I guess. That was why he turned ratty and wouldn't just say.*

*Not long after, he went off out as per usual. So then it was television, and then bedtime. But I didn't feel all that sleepy at first, so I'm writing my diary.*

*We reckon we'll go down to the internet cafe to-morrow, and look Faraday up on the internet. I've some stuff of my own I need to look up for my school holiday project, so we can do both, right?*

*So now I'm going to sleep.*

*Maybe we'll get to see Sean tomorrow, too?*

*Wouldn't that be brill!*

Nora tucked her diary safely away in the inner pocket of her jacket, and went to sleep.

# Chapter Twenty Five

The next day they went to the internet cafe.

This was a small city centre business, with just about room to contain the eight or nine computers round the walls, each with its own work-space.

The counter was at the far end, with a small kitchen opening off behind it. There was a sandwich toaster on the counter, and machines for serving soft drinks on draft, and an old fashioned cash register.

There was also a youngish man of about thirty, with a friendly grin.

He was mainly expert in computer software, with a bit of hardware expertise thrown in, but he was ready to serve up slightly burnt toast, or cheese or ham toasties with the best of them, and to dispense drinks as requested.

It was all part of the loot production which was going to make him, he was convinced, a millionaire some bright day.

This was the owner, known as 'Bill Gates', and he was a friend of Jik and Nora.

'Bill' wore his mousy fair hair long, had round glasses which he peered over when he looked at you, and dressed in torn jeans and tee-shirts which carried elaborate hand painted designs based on mandelbrot patterns.

They sat round drinking coke and chatting for a while.

'Got some cool new games, lads,' Bill told them. 'I'll book you a turn, Jik, if you wanna try them.'

'Hey, cool!' was Jik's immediate response.

Nora was not very pleased. They hadn't come there to play games.

Still, it would cheer Jik up, she supposed.

Of course, as Jik insisted afterwards, what they should have done was enter the name, 'Faraday', in the search engine, straight away, and see what century he lived in.

But Nora had some things she needed to check for her school project.

When she had printed out everything she needed, Jik was keen to try the new games Bill had mentioned – 'I'll only be a minute' – and before they had realised it their time was up, and neither of them had any more money.

'I gave nearly all mine to Captain Julius, and then I got the chips last night,' Jik explained gloomily.

'Right, you did. And I used up mine on the bus here, and buying you that new compass, and the coke we had, and paying for the half hour on the internet that we've just wasted!' realised Nora. 'Hey, you know what, Jik? We'll have to wait till we have more cash before we can check on Faraday, and what's more, we'll have to walk home!'

'Maybe Bill would let us have a go for free?' suggested Jik.

'Yeah, right!' Nora said. 'You know Bill never lets anyone on free or on the 'play now, pay later' system. He says he doesn't want to end up broke instead of making his million. Come back tomorrow, that's his motto.'

As they stood gloomily considering their prospects, the café door pushed open.

It was Bridie Gallagher.

She looked just the same, with her dark hair pushed back in untidy, curly strands, which regularly fell forward over her face, and her cheerful grin.

She went over to the counter, not seeing either Jik or Nora.

'Hi, bro,' she greeted Bill Gates. 'How you doin'?'

Jik's jaw dropped open.

'Bridie!' he exclaimed.

Bridie Gallagher swung round, saw Jik and Nora, and smiled in a friendly way.

'Well, look who's here! Good to see you, lads!'

'So, you know my big sister, then?' Bill said. 'Cool!'

Now that they knew about it, they could both see the resemblance.

'Yeah,' stammered Jik.

'Brendan runs an ace outfit here, right?' Bridie remarked. 'Computers run in our family – like noses.'

'Oh, Bridie's the whiz kid round here,' Bill grinned. 'Makes rings round me when it comes to the old IT. Been writing programs since she stopped sucking her dummy – or maybe before!'

# Chapter 25

Nora said nothing. If Jik wanted to fraternise with the enemy, that was up to him.

But she was surprised to find that Bridie was related to Bill, who had always seemed a really nice guy.

The other three were laughing and talking together. Nora swung round to face the blank screen with its demand to, 'Insert more money'. She pretended to be very busy reading her printouts.

Presently she heard a voice in her ear.

'Bridie came in to pick up Bill and drop him home,' said Jik. 'And she says it's no problem to drop us off, too. So come on.'

Nora trailed miserably out of the café behind them.

Later she commented to Jik, 'It's a wonder you didn't borrow money from that awful Bridie Gallagher for the computer as well as scrounging a lift home.'

'Well, did you want to walk?' asked Jik reasonably. 'Besides, she's not so awful.'

'Yes, she is!' flared Nora.

'I think she'd have liked us to ask her in,' mused Jik. 'But I wasn't going to, with you in that mood. I guess she must have seen from your face that it wouldn't be a good idea'

'I should think not,' Nora said.

'I think she really does like the Da,' Jik went on unwisely. 'Maybe she could help him a bit.'

'Dream on!' Nora was scarlet with anger and misery.

'Well, let's not have a row about it,' Jik said.

They were sitting at the kitchen table, eating toast, and waiting for sounds of Colm getting up. In the background they could hear the toilet flushing. Then heavy footsteps stumbling across to his bedroom. 'Listen, here comes the Da now. As soon as he's had some food, we'll have to tap him for some more cash.'

But it was one of Colm's nights for disappearing as soon as he was up and dressed, and not showing up again until the small hours.

Grabbing the last two slices of toast, and swallowing a mouthful of coffee, he hurried on out of the kitchen with a vague, 'See you later, lads!' and a brief wave of the hand.

The slam of the front door cut short Jik's agonised, 'But, Da –!'

'I'm not going to waste tomorrow again,' said Jik firmly, as they made their way up to bed at one o'clock, with still no sign of Colm. 'We wasted yesterday and today. Tomorrow let's just get down to the marina early, and not hang about waiting for him to get up. And let's not waste any more time at libraries, or internet cafes, either. Today would have been brill for going out on *Lady Molly,* and I bet tomorrow will be, too.'

'How can we go when we've no money to pay for the DART?' asked the practical Nora.

'We'll get it off the Da. I'll go in and ask him for it tomorrow morning, and if he wakes up at all it'll just be to say, 'Sure, take what you need from my pocket,' right?'

'Okay, I guess so,' agreed Nora. 'As long as you definitely ask him, okay, and don't just pinch it.'

'What do you think I am?' retorted Jik virtuously. 'It'll be cool, you'll see. Hey, Nora, it has to be my turn tomorrow. What do you say we try going back to meet Grania? You know – the female pirate who lived in the time of Queen Elizabeth 1?'

Nora's eyes shone. 'That sounds great, Jik! A female pirate – I'd really like to see what she was like!'

Then she hesitated.

'But do you think she was the right century?'

'Why not?' Jik said loftily. 'The school history programme said last term that the Tudor age was the start of modern times – so how about that?'

Nora hesitated no longer.

To tell the truth, she was lit up at the prospect of finding out about a woman who was so famous, and had done so much herself, without being a hanger-on of some important man.

Maybe she could learn something from her.

Nora didn't exactly want to be a pirate.

But she really, really didn't want to be just some dumb girl letting her brother make all the running.

She wanted to do something important with her life.

'Right!' she said briskly. 'Grania it is. Cool. And tomorrow, as early as we can get up!'

# Chapter Twenty Six

It was another bright, sparkling day.

Jik's raid on Colm proved successful.

Tiptoeing into the bedroom, Jik looked in some disgust at the sprawling figure half hidden under the duvet, his face mostly covered by flopping hair.

'Can we have some pocket money, Da?' he asked in his normal voice. Not too loud. He didn't want Colm to actually wake up – just surface enough to agree without really taking it in.

Colm groaned, and flung out one arm.

'Can we have some pocket money, Da?' repeated Jik. 'I can get some out of your jacket, if you like.'

Colm made an effort and opened one eye. He saw Jik's anxious face peering at him.

'Wha'?'

'Pocket money. I can get it myself, if you want.'

'Yeah, right,' Colm mumbled. He extended one hand vaguely. 'Jacket – over there.'

'Thanks, Da.'

The jacket was lying on the floor where Colm had dropped it when he staggered up to bed the night before. Jik felt cautiously in the right hand pocket.

Good. There was plenty of cash. He took a moderate handful, enough for the DART and a bit over.

'Ta, Da.'

As quietly as he had come, he left the room. A moment later, Colm was snoring again.

Then it was the bus, the DART, and making their way along the front at Howth beside the sparkling sea, to the gates of the marina.

'I wish we had been able to get hold of Sean,' Nora said suddenly. She patted her jacket pocket to make sure her diary was safe. The diary and Sean were closely connected in her mind. The diary was so full of her thoughts about him.

'Well, we tried.' Jik sounded unconcerned.

'I know. But maybe we could have gone back later.'

'Well, you know we tried phoning him last night, and nobody answered,' said Jik.

'We could have tried again this morning.'

Jik grunted. He was hoping for the marina gate to open, to give them a chance to slip in. Sometimes it was left open during the day, but other times, like now, it was firmly fastened.

'I think he wants to be friends,' Nora went on. 'You wouldn't think he would be shy, but I think he is. We could have invited him to come with us, today.'

Jik didn't particularly want to talk about it. 'Maybe he'll be there again. When we go back in time, I mean.'

'I hope so. Then we can make sure we have a proper talk. We don't even know if it works the same way for him as for us, or anything.'

'Look,' interrupted Jik suddenly. 'There's Danny Griffiths and his wife. Probably going down to see the *Emerald*. If we catch up with them, they'll let us in – they'll think we're with the Da.'

Breaking into a trot, they came up with the Griffiths, and were automatically taken through the gates with them, according to plan.

'Hi, kids!' Danny Griffiths greeted them jovially. 'Going down to join Colm on *Lady Molly?* I must pop round. I haven't seen the old rascal for yonks.'

'He's not here yet,' Jik said hastily. 'We came on ahead. He's getting some stuff.'

Nora, who didn't like lying, said nothing, and went rather red.

'Well, I must catch up with him soon,' Danny Griffiths said. 'Give him my regards, right?'

Then he peeled off down the side pontoon, leaving Jik and Nora to breathe sighs of relief as they scuttled on down to where, in the bright sunshine and the fresh breeze, *Lady Molly* bobbed welcomingly at her mooring.

There was no sign of The Snapper.

They climbed on board and settled down to wait for him.

Jik unlocked the cabin door.

'Shall I make a cup of tea?' suggested Nora. Cooking on board *Lady Molly* was so different from cooking at home. She somehow never thought of it as a girlie thing to be avoided.

# Chapter 26

'Good idea,' agreed Jik. 'Hey, we should have brought some bread, and I could have made toast! But, sure, there won't be any milk for tea.'

'Neither there will.' Nora groaned with disappointment.

Jik was poking in the cupboard under the small worktop. In a moment he emerged triumphantly.

'Cuppa Soup! I was pretty sure there'd be some. We can make that!'

'Dead on!' agreed Nora. 'I'll stick the kettle on, if you put some into mugs.'

Ten minutes later, they were sitting on the cabin roof, taking occasional cautious sips at the boiling hot soup, and letting it cool in the fresh breeze.

'I wonder if The Snapper means to come at all?' Nora asked after a while. 'Did we do any unselfish acts last time?'

'Well, we tried to rescue Maewyn from the captain,' retorted Jik. 'That was unselfish, wasn't it?'

'Certainly it was!' said a cheerful voice in their ears.

It was The Snapper himself, making his way along the narrow side deck to hoist himself up on the cabin roof beside them.

'Ahoy, shipmates! Any of that soup going for an old sailor man?'

'You can have this, and I'll get some more for myself,' offered Nora, scrambling down eagerly.

As soon as she was in the cabin, The Snapper spoke quietly to Jik. 'However, there are other rules, Jik my lad. Those lies you told to Danny Griffiths. They didn't exactly help your case.'

Jik went scarlet. 'I suppose not, Snapper,' he said in a miserable voice. 'Does that mean we can't go? Have I blown it?'

The Snapper smiled kindly. 'It's all right for this time, Jik,' he said. 'But I have to warn you that lies don't just float off into space. They'll come back on you soon. So make sure you don't add to them, right?'

'Right,' agreed Jik. He still felt quite miserable.

But just then, Nora reappeared with her soup, and the subject was dropped. The Snapper, Jik realised with gratitude, wasn't going to tell him off in front of anyone else, even Nora.

'Well, my lads,' began The Snapper cheerfully, when they had all finished their soup, and the mugs had been tidily rinsed and left to drain on the worktop, 'so where are we heading for this bright and beautiful day?'

'It's Jik's turn,' Nora said.

'Well, Jik?'

'We thought we'd like to try the time of Grania Ni Mhaille.' Jik said. 'She was a female pirate, round about the time of the Spanish Armada. I know the sailors and explorers then made all sorts of new discoveries, so I thought –' his voice trailed off.

'You thought it would be exciting, eh, Jik?' The Snapper said shrewdly. 'And you're both agreed on this?'

Nora nodded.

'Fair enough,' said The Snapper. 'But if you don't mind a word of advice, I wouldn't waste too many turns. We can't go on forever, you know. Next time, try to make sure it's the right time!'

Jik and Nora looked at each other.

'Not too late to change your minds!' said The Snapper. 'No? Well, here we go, then. Let's get this boat under way.'

The familiar and yet exciting routine of taking the boat out to sea went ahead. Then, just as he had done twice before, The Snapper said, 'Hold tight!'

Then there was darkness, and the abrupt pitching of the boat.

# Chapter Twenty Seven

This time it was still dark when the boat stopped pitching.

The ship they were suddenly on seemed, as far as they could tell, to be much larger than *Lady Molly*.

Larger, too, than either of the previous ships they had visited.

And although the pitching of the time travel had stopped, they were rolling steadily, with an unfamiliar motion.

Although it was dark, the ship was brightly lit. There were lamps fore and aft, and many bright lights from what seemed to be a number of cabins both forward and amidships.

Moreover, the superstructure was built up to a considerable height, so that it seemed to overhang them in an awe inspiring way.

'Wow!' muttered Jik. 'Some craft, Nora!'

'Is it a Spanish galleon, do you think?'

'Well, not Spanish, stupid. But a sort of galleon, I guess.'

They looked around them, trying to get their bearings.

'What do you think we should do, Jik?' Nora asked. 'Hide, or speak to someone?'

'No point in hiding,' said Jik sensibly. 'We need to be able to ask about old Peter's invention.'

'Yeah,' agreed Nora reluctantly. To tell the truth, she was finding this particular adventure more frightening than the others. Perhaps because she felt very small in the big ship.

'We should get one of the crew to take us to Grania,' Jik went on. ''Take me to your leader' – right?'

'Right.'

They looked round for a suitable crew member.

A roughly dressed boy, not much older than Jik, was coiling a rope nearby.

Jik went over to him.

'Hey, how ya doing?' he began easily. 'We need to speak to your captain. To Grania, I mean.'

The boy stared at him. He looked more alarmed than Nora, so that she felt some confidence growing.

'I have to sort these ropes,' he muttered. 'Captain'll be at the helm.'

'Right,' Jik said briskly. 'So where's the helm, then?'

The boy looked surprised, but didn't dare to question him. 'Up there.'

'Ta.'

'Up there' was a looming construction at the end of a steep companionway, aft of where Jik and Nora were standing.

Jik, seeing that Nora was hesitating to move forward, took her firmly by the arm and headed for the foot of the ladder.

'Up we go!' he said, and began to climb.

Nora followed.

The raised deck was a solid structure, but not very large. It had room for perhaps four people in comfort.

At the moment it held only one. But that one seemed enough to occupy the whole area.

A gigantic figure stood astride the deck, one arm holding the tiller, head thrown back and a bright red silk scarf tied around the flowing hair. Short sword stuck through the broad leather belt. High shiny boots, bright green shirt and short dark trousers, tucked into the boots.

Hearing Jik at the top of the ladder, the figure swung round, one hand feeling for the sword.

'Well?' boomed a fierce voice. 'What is it? Trouble?'

Then the eyes narrowed.

'Who are you? I don't know you?'

At first Jik had taken the huge figure for a man. Now, hearing her voice, he realised that this was a woman – Grania Ni Mhaille, fiercest and most successful of all Ireland's sea captains. Renowned throughout England as well as Ireland. Acknowledged by Elizabeth of England. Allowed to roam free and granted the right to bear arms against all England's enemies by sea and land.

'Hail, Grania!' he said. 'We are travellers from beyond the mists of time, come to do honour to the renowned queen of Ireland, and to seek wisdom from your knowledge of the seas.'

Nora gasped. This was going for it with a vengeance! What would Grania say?

But the female pirate threw back her head and laughed.

# Chapter 27

'By thunder, I stand amazed. Travellers in time! Workers of strong magic, then! But you do not look it. Come forward to me. Let me look at you!'

They stepped forward. Now the bright lanterns swinging above the helm shone directly into their faces.

Grania stared at them shrewdly.

'Hm. Young enough, to be workers of mighty magic,' she commented.

'Our age doesn't matter!' burst out Nora. 'We have been sent by someone more powerful than ourselves. More powerful even than you, Grania!'

The pirate captain threw back her head and laughed again.

'I see that, young or not, you have no fear of speaking your minds,' she said. 'Tell me your names, since you make so free with mine.'

'I am Jik,' Jik said. Then, remembering their previous experience with Cuchulain, he went on hastily, 'of the clan of Lavery, from Dublin. And this is my sister Nora.'

'A girl!' Grania exclaimed. 'And, by my troth, a girl dressed sensibly for the sea, as I am myself. I've never seen that before! I thought no woman but myself wore the trews. This is good to see, indeed!'

She relaxed against the wheel, one mighty arm still controlling its motion.

'So, Jik and Nora, tell me more. What is this mission on which, you say, you are sent? But, wait. I am forgetting my manners. Travellers should be greeted well, with rest, and food and drink. Let me take you down to my cabin, and I will see what we have to offer you.'

'Great,' agreed Jik enthusiastically. 'And maybe you'll tell us some stories about yourself?'

'We'd love to hear all about your adventures,' Nora added earnestly.

Grania threw back her head and gave her great ringing laugh again.

'Perhaps!' she said. 'But, now, I must call for my mate to take over the tiller. Wait there.'

She picked up a large brass gong and a padded hammer, and beat loudly. Almost at once they heard sounds of approaching footsteps climbing the ladder.

A head popped over the edge of the companionway, then a roughly dressed sailor scrambled up onto the deck.

Nora looked at him carefully. But he was no one she had ever seen before.

Grania clapped her hands together and issued a string of orders. In no time at all, the mate – a man only slightly less impressive than Grania herself – had appeared to take over control of the ship's course, and Grania was leading them to her cabin, at the stern of the ship.

# Chapter Twenty Eight

Inside the cabin were more bright lights. Looking round, Nora realised that comfort, even luxury, aboard ship had come on considerably since St Patrick's time – at least for the important people.

The cabin had large windows on both sides. Cushions were sprawled along the seating, both to port and to starboard. The woodwork was painted in gilt, and on one wall was an oil painting of a fierce looking man in the prime of life. Grania's father, Owen O'Malley, known as the Black Oak, they discovered presently.

Jik was more interested in the broad table placed in the centre of the available space, and piled with fruit, roast chicken, wine in a sparkling decanter, gold plates, and some things which they learned were sweetmeats – the equivalent of cakes and pastries.

'Wow!' he said faintly.

'Jik, Nora – be seated, my friends. First we will satisfy your bodily needs, then the requirements of the mind,' Grania smiled. She waved them to the cushioned benches. She herself took a chair, carved with grapes and vine-leaves, with wide arms and a scarlet cushion trimmed with gold.

Then she began to carve the chicken, using a sharp knife which hung from her belt, half obscured by the sword they had noticed earlier.

Nora looked with interest at the chicken placed before her on a gold plate. She looked around her for knife and fork. There was no sign of either.

Jik, seeing what she was doing, winked furiously at her.

Clearly there was only one knife – Grania's own. Perhaps people were expected to supply their own handy knife in their belt if they wanted to use one. It would probably be considered very rude if Nora started asking for one.

Picking up a piece of chicken in his hands, Jik said, 'Just like *Kentucky Fried Chicken*, right, Nora? Finger lickin' good!'

Grania, although not entirely clear what he was saying, realised that Jik was complimenting the food.

She smiled graciously.

Nora, getting the hint, picked up some chicken in turn and bit off a good mouthful. Grania poured them some wine, and passed the other dishes.

To Jik and Nora, it was a strange feast, but certainly a good one.

They bombarded the female pirate with questions, and, laughing loudly, she answered as much as she cared to.

'So, is this a galleon?' Nora asked at one point.

'No. This is a war galley,' Grania told them. 'I remember my first ship, not exactly a galleon, but a caravel, many years ago now. It was a mighty ship, and I almost burst with pride the first time I took her out. My father, Owen O'Malley, bought her for me. He was a mighty man of the sea, looked up to by his people for many miles around, and at that time the only thing I wanted was to be like him.

'I can never be grateful enough to my father. When he saw how much I loved the sea, instead of standing in my way, and keeping me at home like other girl children, he took me with him on his trading voyages, taught me how to handle a ship as soon as I could reach the helm, taught me never to be fearful or to shrink from danger.

'Perhaps if he had had sons to come after him, it would have been different. I think I was the son he never had.

'I did my best to repay him for his kindness, as soon as I was old enough to understand it. I worked to become the best at everything to do with sailing and the sea.

'Then, on a proud day, he gave me my first caravel, and I sailed her, with a worthy crew, in search of adventure.

'Many the rich merchant ship I plundered, many the treasure loads of gold or goods, wool, tallow, weapons, which I brought home and shared with him.

'Alas, my poor ship!

'No one really knows how it happened. But I think, from what some of my crew told me, it was like this.

'There came a day when one of the crewmen broke the strict rule and took some live coals from the cooking fire, put them in a warming pan, and carried them on deck with him during his watch, hidden under his cloak. He had been ill, but did not want to miss the voyage and his share of the plunder. So, like a fool, he tried to keep himself warm, and spilled a live coal among some ropes. By the time anyone knew what was happening, or the alert had been given, the ship was well alight.

'My crewmen were brave. Side by side with me, they fought the flames, and all might yet have been well, if it had not been that, at that moment, God sent a storm. The caravel was so damaged that it could never hope to survive in such heavy seas.

'Even so, I would have tried. I sent my crew, especially the injured, ashore in the ship's galleys – the life boats – and I would have stayed aboard, alone, to sail my caravel to safety.

'But, alas, a falling spar hit me on the head, or so I am told, for I remember nothing of it.

'My mate carried me over his shoulder to the waiting galley. Thank God he was a big, strong man! Even so, it taxed all his strength! I am no lightweight!

'And when I came back to consciousness, it was to see my lovely ship sinking beneath the waves.'

Grania sighed with the remembered grief.

'But all your crew were rescued?' Nora asked.

'Indeed.' Grania smiled. 'That was something to be thankful for.'

'And you got another caravel?' Jik asked.

'I did. But my first caravel – she was special. I'll always regret losing her.'

Then, putting off her grief, she laughed her hearty laugh. 'Now I have the best ship of them all, my flagship, my *Seabird*. Isn't she a beauty?

'But, come, my friends. This is unfair. I have told you story after story, and you have said nothing about this mysterious mission of yours. What is it you would ask of me?'

Jik took a deep breath.

'We know, Grania, that this is the age of discovery. New lands, new inventions. We have an ancestor, Peter Lavery, who made a discovery which is of the greatest importance to the ships and sailors of our own day.' He paused, marshalling his thoughts.

'Well?' asked Grania. 'Tell me more.'

'Peter made this discovery. But instead of getting the credit for it, he lost out big time.'

'I don't understand,' Grania said.

'Well, no one really knows that he invented this idea. Other people followed it up, but Peter never got any acknowledgement for his part.'

'I see,' said Grania slowly. 'But what is this discovery? And how do you think I can help you?'

'It's a way of sailing ships when there's nothing else, no stars or anything, to help. We thought, since you know so much about the sea, you might know about Peter's invention, and you might be able to tell us more about it,' Nora burst out. 'We really wanted someone who would sign something to say that it was Peter who discovered the fore-runner to radar.'

Grania stared at them. An angry frown began to build up on her face.

At last she spoke.

'And you think that I – I, Grania Ni Mhaille – have had some part in stealing this idea of your ancestor's? Or worse still, you have come, not from another time, but from another country, to steal some of our discoveries for yourselves? So that, when you fight our ships, we will no longer have the advantage of you in sea battle?'

As she spoke, Grania was gradually working herself up into a towering rage.

'This discovery you speak of – it sounds like our compass. And perhaps your sailors know nothing of this, and you want to steal the idea from us?'

She glared at them.

'No, no, Grania, it's not like that at all!' Jik tried hurriedly to explain. 'We already know all about compasses. We don't need to steal your secrets. We really are from the future. We have a thing called radar to steer our ships with. I suppose it mustn't have been invented until centuries after your time. We just hoped –' He faltered, not sure how to explain himself.

'We thought Peter might be someone you knew,' Nora put in. 'A friend, right? Someone whose invention you might have heard of?'

'Someone whose invention I might have stolen?' Grania cut in swiftly. She sprang to her feet, one hand on her sword. 'And with my meat and salt in your mouths, you would accuse me of treachery? You deserve to be hurled overboard!'

'No, no,' gasped Jik. 'We certainly aren't accusing you of anything. We just wanted your help!'

# Chapter 28

But it was too late.

With a furious shout of 'Fergus! Kevin!' Grania was already summoning the nearest crewmen.

'Take these villains and lock them in the brig!' she ordered fiercely, as two sturdy sailors hurried into the cabin. 'I don't want to see them again until morning.'

She swung back to Jik and Nora.

'If you had not already supped well with my food, I would put you on bread and water while you think out your position,' she said angrily. 'I, also, need to think. To devise a fitting punishment for two spies and liars. Take them away, Kevin!'

And Jik and Nora were dragged, protesting, from the cabin, to be thrown into a dark space below decks. As Fergus dragged her along, twisting one arm up behind her back painfully, Nora saw a crowd of grinning sailors to one side, watching them.

Something went ding inside her head. That man – the richly dressed man in the colourful dark blue silks, and the purple velvet cloak. He was tall and sturdy, and he stood apart from the rest, his hand hiding the lower part of his face. Surely she'd see him before?

But there was no time to think about it. Fergus, letting go of Nora's arm, pushed her roughly through a dark doorway. She stumbled forward. Beside her, Jik was receiving the same treatment from Kevin. There was no chance to fight back.

Despairing, they heard the slam of the thick oak door, and the sound of a heavy key turning in the lock

'Oh, Jik!' whispered Nora, in a voice not far from tears.

Jik sat down on the bare floor boards and leant his head in his hands.

'This is just about the utter end,' he said.

# Chapter Twenty Nine

Inside the brig – the prison quarters – it was very dark. Jik and Nora could not see each other. Nora stretched out one hand, and touched Jik's arm. Then she moved her hand cautiously along his arm until she could take hold of his hand. It helped a lot.

'Oh, Jik!' she said again. 'What do you think she'll do to us?'

'Well, she's a pirate,' said Jik gloomily. 'She'll likely make us walk the plank.'

Then he felt Nora's hand quiver, and went on hastily, 'No, no, I don't see why she would do that.'

'Why didn't she believe us, Jik? No one else thought we were lying.'

Jik swallowed hard.

'I was wondering that.'

Then he got up his courage, and said, 'Maybe because of the lies I told Danny Griffiths to get us through the marina gate. Snapper said it would come back on me. I suppose if you go round telling lies, you shouldn't be surprised if people take you for a liar. Even when you happen to be telling the truth.'

Nora said nothing. She squeezed Jik's hand.

'I'm just sorry it's come back on you as well, Nora.'

'Well,' Nora pointed out, 'it was as much my fault as yours, because I went along with what you said, and was just as glad that Danny Griffiths believed you, right?'

'Snapper didn't think it was your fault,' Jik insisted. Since he felt so guilty, he was almost glad to shoulder all the blame himself.

'Meanwhile,' said Nora, suddenly her practical self, 'how are we going to get out of here?'

'Kick down the door,' said Jik, abruptly feeling light hearted again, with his confession made and done with. 'Steal one of the galleys. Fight off the crew when they try to stop us launching it. Row to the nearest land, where we'll find ourselves transported home again!'

'Okay, Arnie. Or we could just say, 'Beam me up, Scotty',' agreed Nora. 'But, seriously.'

'I haven't a clue.'

They sat quietly side by side and thought.

'People often escape by burning down the door,' Nora suggested presently. 'Have you a lighter?'

'Yeah. But you remember that story she told us. I wouldn't really want to wreck the whole ship, and maybe get the crew either burned or drowned. And I quite like Grania, even if she did throw us in here. It wouldn't be cool to destroy the *Seabird*. She really loves it.'

'Right,' agreed Nora. 'We couldn't do that to her.'

'And we might get burnt or drowned ourselves.'

'Yeah, right.'

They sat quietly some more.

Through the locked door they could hear the sounds of the ship.

A creaking of timbers.

Occasional shouts from one crewman to another.

Bursts of wind in the canvas.

After a while, they drifted off into sleep.

Hours later, they were wakened by the suddenly increased noise.

There were feet running, loud shouts, the sound of the gong and shrill whistles.

'Wha –? Wha –?' mumbled Nora sleepily.

'Dunno.' Jik was quicker to wake fully.

'Something's happening. Hush. Listen.'

Nora sat up and listened carefully.

They could hear a loud thumping sound, as if something – or more than one something – was being dragged across the deck. Someone was bellowing out orders.

Remembering Grania's story, and their own discussion of means of escape, she wondered confusedly if the warship was on fire.

But, no. Surely she would smell the fire and the smoke.

Was it a storm?

Were they launching the lifeboats? The galleys, she corrected herself.

The ship was rolling no more and no less than before. It couldn't be a storm, or they would feel the pitching and tossing.

There seemed to be no real panic, as far as Jik and Nora could tell. No one was shrieking or wailing.

# Chapter 29

Just shouts, orders, the noise of a furious activity.

Among the shouts, Nora thought she could distinguish a few words.

'Enemy ship!'

'All hands on deck!'

Then, a few moments later, something about cannon.

'Man the cannon!' – was that it?

There were sounds as if something heavy was being dragged along the deck.

Jik was jumping with excitement.

'Nora! I bet we're attacking a treasure ship! Isn't this brill!'

'I don't think it's brill at all,' Nora said. The reality of it had suddenly come home to her. 'They'll probably kill people.'

Jik ignored her. 'I wish we were outa here. I wish we could join in!'

Nora shuddered.

'Perhaps this would be a good chance to get away,' she wondered aloud. 'They'll all be too busy to think of us.'

'Yeah. If we could get the door open,' Jik reminded her.

'Oh, right.'

And then they heard the voice at the door.

'Jik? Nora? Are you in there?'

They stared at each other unbelievingly for a moment.

Then Jik spoke.

'Yes – we're here. Who are you?'

'It's me, you fool,' said the voice.

'Laeg ! Marcus! I mean Sean!' Nora gasped. 'Is it really you?'

They heard a brief laugh. 'Yeah – but I'm Diarmid this time round. One of Grania's most trusted crewmen.'

'Wow!'

'Cool!'

'No time for chat,' said 'Diarmid'. 'I got the key from the mate while he was on the watch below. Sleeping, I mean.'

They heard the grating noise of the heavy key as it turned in the lock.

# Chapter Thirty

They pushed the huge door open, Diarmid helping.

There he was, dressed in the same rough gear they had seen on the other crewmen, ragged shirt tucked into woollen trews cut off at the knee, a scarf tied round his hair, a few fair strands falling into his eyes as usual.

Nora could have wept with joy to see him. Jik, though less emotional about it, acknowledged to himself that he was pretty pleased.

'Quiet, now,' Diarmid warned them. 'Follow me, and don't dare make a sound.'

Creeping silently along the deck, easily able to keep from making much noise in their trainers, Jik and Nora could hardly believe what was happening.

Soon they came to a companionway.

Diarmid stopped. He turned to them, a finger to his lips.

'This takes us to the starboard side, the opposite side of the ship from the Spanish vessel,' he explained. 'Even so, in case there are some men about, I'll go first and check. Don't show your heads until I say.'

So they had been right. The noise and bustle was an attack being mounted on an enemy ship, to port, as they had thought.

At that second, the first of the cannon balls was fired. Then another.

The sound was devastating. Nora clapped her hands over her ears, and saw that Jik was doing the same.

There was a pause for reloading. Then came the 'Boom! Boom!' again.

Two cannons, Jik thought.

Diarmid had disappeared, swarming swiftly up the ladder and then moving out of their sight.

Jik started up after him, stopping with his head below deck level. Nora followed.

Diarmid's voice came quietly down to them.

'Right. Come on now.'

Quickly they scrambled on up, and followed Diarmid across the deck to the shelter of a long galley roped to the starboard side.

'The plan is to get this launched while no one's noticing,' Diarmid said quietly. 'If we can manage that, we lower ourselves into it and row away as quietly and quickly as possible. It's a dark night, so that will help.'

'But what about the splash when it drops into the sea?' asked Nora.

'We time it to be covered by the cannon, of course!' said Jik quickly. 'Cool idea, man!'

'Let's get started,' Diarmid said. 'There won't be many more cannonballs fired, unless they've all been misses. And that's not likely, with Grania's crew. They'll be moving on to the grappling irons soon. Pulling the ship over. Then boarding her, for hand to hand fighting.'

'How much longer, do you think?' Jik asked.

'Dunno. Time enough. So – let's get on.'

They began quickly to cast off the ropes which held the galley in place. Like modern lifeboats, it was held at or above rail height, to make it easier to put it overboard in a crisis.

Jik and Nora were good at ropes and knots. So, they soon realised, was Diarmid. They were nearly ready when footsteps sounded along the deck.

'Quick – climb up and duck down inside the boat!' ordered Diarmid softly.

Jik and Nora were quick to obey.

They crouched down, the boat swaying slightly with their weight.

Diarmid strolled along the deck towards the approaching sailor.

'Fergus,' he greeted him. 'What you doing over here away from the fighting?'

'Diarmid. How ya doing?' Fergus responded. He was one of the big, burly crewmen who had dragged Jik and Nora to the brig, on Grania's orders. 'Captain sent me to check on the prisoners.'

Diarmid laughed, and Nora admired how cool he sounded.

'Typical of the bosses!' he said. 'The mate sent me on the same task. Talk about wasted effort, when they need every man for the fight. Well, at least I can save you the time. They're both safe nd sound. What were you going to do for a key, by the way, since the mate gave it to me?'

'I never thought of that!' Fergus grinned. 'Captain must have thought it would be in the door. Well, we'd best be getting back, then.'

He took Diarmid's arm and walked away with him along the deck.

'Hey! What will Diarmid do now?' Nora moaned.

'He'll slip back as soon as he can,' Jik said firmly. 'Meantime, let's get on with this galley.'

In a very short time the boat was free and ready to push overboard.

'What are we to do?' Nora worried. 'We should launch the galley next time we hear the first cannon fire. We can't afford to wait, and find they've stopped firing. But I don't want us to go without Sean!'

'Of course. There's no way we're going without him. But that doesn't stop us from launching the galley, and being ready.'

'We'll need to be sure and keep hold of a rope each, to keep it from drifting away.'

'Right.'

They scrambled down from the boat, took firm hold of a rope each, and positioned themselves to be ready to push at the right moment.

Soon came the roar of the first cannon.

'Push!' said Jik.

They put out all their strength. Just as the second cannon boomed, the galley slid smoothly over the rail.

The splash as it hit the water could hardly be heard, even by Jik and Nora standing directly above it, for the echoing roar of the cannon.

'Wow, that was something!' Jik said. 'Got your rope okay, Nora?'

'Got it.' Nora had just about enough breath left for her answer.

'So. Now all we have to do is wait for Sean to come back.'

They settled down to wait.

Time limped slowly by.

'Jik,' said Nora presently. 'Should one of us go and see what's happening?'

'I don't know,' said Jik. 'If we get caught, it wrecks the whole plan. We can't both go, right. One of us needs to hold on to the rope.'

'Yeah, that's why I said one of us!' Nora retorted. 'And it had better be me. I couldn't hold onto the whole weight of the galley myself.'

'But perhaps he expected us just to go on by ourselves?' worried Jik. 'He's safe enough, after all. He doesn't need to escape. Grania thinks well of him, from what he said.'

'But don't you see?' Nora almost forgot to keep her voice down. 'He's blown it, now! He told Fergus that the mate gave him the key, and that the prisoners were both safe and sound –'

'– and so we are! –'

'– yeah, right, but they're bound to find out that he took the key without permission, and that since we aren't still locked in, he must have let us out. And then he'll be in big trouble!'

'Yeah, major league!' agreed Jik.

'Okay,' he said after a moment's thought. 'Here's what we'll do. I'll find something to tie my end of the rope to. You keep hold of yours. Then you can stay here, in case he comes back while I'm away looking for him. I'll be the one to go. And no argument.'

'Okay.'

Jik fastened his rope securely to the rail.

Then moving as quietly as possible, he slipped like a shadow along the deck, in search of their friend.

# Chapter Thirty One

On the port side of *Seabird,* the noise level was still just as high.

The crewmen were milling around in crowds, sorting out grappling irons, preparing to board the now badly damaged Spanish galleon.

Jik, keeping out of sight behind masts and bulkheads, looked for any sign of 'Diarmid'.

There he was, still with Fergus.

But something was wrong.

Fergus had hold of Diarmid by the arm. A strong hold, impossible to break.

Beside them stood a man who looked familiar to Jik. A tall, sturdy man, dressed in silks and velvets.

Jik wriggled forward, desperate to make out the words. The familiar looking man seemed to be giving Fergus instructions.

'I tell you I saw him myself!' he snapped at Fergus. 'He had the key, and as I watched I saw him turn it in the lock of the brig door. Then he and the prisoners between them pushed it open, and all three of them ran off to starboard. I was too far off to prevent them, so I hurried to find someone to help me catch them again. And then I came across you, with the boldest ruffian of the lot, treating him as a friend. Grania needs to hear of this, my man!'

'All right, all right!' Fergus mumbled. 'If you're sure? Diarmid, have you any explanation for this fellow's story?'

'You know me, Fergus,' Diarmid began. 'Do you really believe this stranger instead of your own mate?'

Fergus looked doubtful. Then his face cleared. 'Tell you what – we'll leave it up to Grania.'

It was the end. As Jik watched, her could see Diarmid decide to make a break for it. It must have seemed his only chance. Seconds later he was pelting along the deck. But he hadn't reckoned on the speed of the stranger's reactions. as Diarmid passed, one foot shot out and Diarmid, tripped cleverly, was sent flying.

Suddenly the position was reversed again. Fergus seized hold of Diarmid. Then he began to stride along the deck, dragging

Diarmid with him, while the other man hurried alongside them, making encouraging motions with his hands.

They were heading, Jik saw, for a group of people over on the port side of the ship. Jik took a deep breath, and hurried after them.

It was difficult enough to keep out of sight. Jik was afraid of losing Diarmid, by keeping too far back, or else being caught, by staying too close.

He hurried across the deck, ducking and dodging behind every bit of cover, and managed to come up with Diarmid and his captors, just before they reached Grania.

The pirate captain stood in her usual position, legs spread apart, one hand on her sword. She was bellowing instructions to a group of men who were struggling to roll the cannons back under cover.

'Put your backs into it, you useless dogs!' her great voice boomed. 'Heave away, lads!'

The man who looked familiar, who had accused and then tripped Diarmid, swept Grania a deep bow, and spoke respectfully.

'Captain,' he began, 'I bring you this traitor, this boy caught by myself in the act of betraying you – '

'What! My bold Diarmid!' roared Grania unbelievingly. 'Diarmid would never betray me! Loose his arm, Fergus.' Fergus reluctantly obeyed, and Jik thought that his moment had come to rescue Diarmid, but almost at the same second Grania herself had seized Diarmid's arm and was shaking it, in a grip at least as strong as that of Fergus.

'What, my trusty boy, would you betray me?' She laughed aloud.

'Alas, Captain, it is only too true!' insisted the man. 'I myself – '

'You! And who are you?' roared Grania.

The mate tugged her sleeve, and Jik could just make out his whisper.

'Passenger with papers for the Queen – to be treated with honour, remember? Cathga, he's called.'

Grania frowned, obviously remembering something distasteful. She clearly disliked having been forced to take a passenger and to treat him with respect. On her own ship, Grania was master. If she choose to carry a passenger, well enough, but to have one forced upon her was another matter.

Still, needs must.

She shrugged, and spoke to Cathga in a more moderate tone. 'I remember you now, Master Diplomat. But I still do not know what this treachery is, of which you accuse my trusty crewman?'

For a moment Cathga's face was lit up as one of the crewmen shone a lantern into his eyes.

And Jik saw clearly. It was the druid priest.

Jik drew another deep breath as Grania turned slightly away from Fergus, still holding Diarmid by the arm, to speak with the diplomat.

It was now or never.

Inflating his lungs, and trying to copy as well as he could the rough accents he had heard from the crew members, he called out, 'Captain! Come quick! The *Seabird's* been hit!'

Grania spun round.

'What? Who's that? The ship hit? Where?'

There was a moment's panic, which gave Jik his chance.

Like a bullet he shot out of hiding, head down, and charged Grania full in the stomach.

Grania, letting go of Diarmid's arm, sat down heavily backwards, the breath knocked out of her.

At first she could do nothing, not even speak.

Seizing Diarmid by the arm, Jik rushed him back into the shadows, heading towards starboard, out of sight of the almost immediate pursuit.

They fled along the deck, trying to combine speed and silence.

They were almost at the stern of the ship.

'Right!' gasped Jik. 'Nothing else for it! Over the side! Go round the stern end. Swim along the starboard side till we reach Nora and the galley!'

'Remember I can't swim!' Diarmid gasped out, trying to run and to answer Jik at the same time.

'Never mind,' Jik said. 'I'll tow you. I can keep you above water. Hope you'll be okay!'

'Me, too.'

'Come on, go for it!'

They climbed the stern rail. There was no time to think.

'One, two, three – jump!'

Over they went, jumping clear, keeping well out from the rudder, flying side by side into the night.

Their heads surfaced. Jik seized Diarmid in the classic life saving position. He kicked his way vigorously along the starboard side of the flagship.

He kept close to the side of the ship. As often as possible he used one hand to gain purchase from the hull, to push them along more quickly.

It was good that Diarmid kept still and didn't add to the difficulties by struggling.

Jik had time to admire his courage. For someone who couldn't swim, it was no joke to jump into the sea, and then trust yourself to someone else like this.

Risking a glance over his shoulder, he saw the dark shape of the galley not far away. On board the *Seabird*, no one seemed to realize what they had done. If Grania was still looking for them, she must be looking on the port side of the ship.

The over-hanging superstructure along the edge of the warship hid them from sight of anyone peering down over the rail. Just as long as they kept close to the side.

Jik was fairly sure no one had realised that they had jumped overboard. If the search for them was still on, and, if Cathga had anything to do with it, he was sure that it would be, then they would still be searching along the deck, among the piles of ropes and other possible cover.

He tried to keep noise and splashes down to a minimum.

Then all at once he felt himself bumping into something, and realised that they had reached the galley.

'Can you help yourself up and into the boat, man?' he asked, puffing from the effort he had been making. 'Grab hold of the edge. I'll try to give you a boost.'

Diarmid scrambled over the edge and into the galley. Then, leaning out, he grasped Jik's shoulders and helped him to scramble on board in his turn.

'Jik! Is that you?' called a voice softly from above.

'Yeah. Let yourself down carefully, Nora. Don't forget to cast off first. I'll try to hold on to the ship, so we won't drift too far out until you're down.'

A couple of ropes snaked quietly down beside them. They hung unto whatever parts of the *Seabird* they could grasp.

A dark shape which was Nora climbed carefully over the bulwark and dropped into the boat.

'Now, push off,' instructed Jik. 'Take one of these oars, Nora. Don't try to row yet – too noisy. We'll paddle quietly for a bit until we're far enough away.'

'I can row, even if I can't swim,' said Diarmid. 'I'll take the other oar.'

'Right.'

Paddling carefully, they took the galley out of earshot of the looming mass of the *Seabird*.

Then it was out oars, and rowing with all their strength until they felt safe enough to rest.

It was still dark. There was no moon, and the overcast sky hid the stars.

'Better get some sleep for now,' suggested Jik. 'We must be well out of sight of the *Seabird* by now. When we can see round us, we can aim for the nearest land.'

'Depends how far away it is,' Diarmid said.

'And if we can even see any,' Nora put in.

'Ah, let's worry about that when it's daylight,' Jik said. He was half asleep by now. 'Anyway, I've got my new compass. Good thing you got round to buying it, Nora.'

Nora nodded. Then she realised that Jik couldn't see her and said, 'Yeah. But we'll need to find land really soon.'

'Come on, stop chattering and get some rest,' ordered Jik. 'We'd better stick to the benches. She's shipping a bit of water. The floor boards will be too damp. Nothing to worry about, mind.'

It wasn't the most comfortable of sleeping quarters, but somehow they curled themselves into the best positions they could manage. Before they had time to think any more about their danger, they had drifted off to sleep.

# Chapter Thirty Two

Nora woke the next morning with the sun in her eyes.

All around the galley stretched miles of empty ocean. The sun, not yet fully risen, sparkled on the calm waters. It was a beautiful day.

Best of all, there was no sign whatever of Grania's flagship. They must have rowed quite a long way during the dark hours. And not, as Nora had been half afraid, round in circles.

Suddenly Nora realised that she was hungry. She sat up, and nudged Jik with her foot.

'Wake up, bro' she said, 'and tell me what we do for breakfast?'

Both boys heard her and woke at the same time.

'There's a thought,' said Jik.

'It's okay,' Diarmid told him. 'All the galleys carry emergency provisions. Not a feast, right, but water and probably ship's biscuits. Stuff that won't go bad.'

'Like, iron rations,' Jik nodded. 'Okay, let's find it.'

'First, are we out of sight of Grania's warship, the *Seabird*?'

Diarmid peered round the open sea carefully.

'Yep, first thing I checked when I woke up,' Nora assured him.

'Yeah. Seem to be.' Jik shrugged. 'Thing is, which way is she, and which way is land?'

'Let's eat first, and worry about that later,' suggested Nora, who had just discovered how thirsty she was as well as hungry.

'Yeah, right.'

'Okay.'

They fished out the water cask and each took a hearty slug.

The dry biscuits were not so pleasant, but Nora discovered a bar of chocolate in her pocket, and divided it scrupulously among them.

'So,' said Jik finally. 'Where do you reckon the nearest land would be, Diarmid?'

'You might as well call me Sean. 'Diarmid' is about blown out. I sure enough don't want to run into the people again who know me as that.'

'Sean.'

'Right. I'm sort of guessing. But Grania set out from Connemara, heading North West. So if we head pretty well east, that should be the best.'

'Well, we'll try it,' Jik decided. 'Can't see what else we can do.'

'If we do find land, that'll be it,' Nora reminded him. 'We'll be straight home.'

'No point in staying here anyway,' Jik said. 'Grania didn't know anything about the invention, and if she doesn't probably no one here does. We must still be going too far back.'

Nora carefully didn't say, 'I told you so.'

Instead, 'What about Sean?' she asked anxiously. 'We don't want to disappear home and leave him here by himself.'

'Don't worry about me,' Sean put in. 'As soon as you guys disappear, Snapper will come for me – at least that's how it's worked the other times.'

'Let's set the compass and start rowing,' Jik said.

He set his compass by the rising sun. It would be east at the moment, but as the day wore on, it would move. So it was difficult to use the sun to steer by. That was why they needed the compass. He remembered the Da teaching him about this when he was only about eight or nine.

He felt a quick pang, as he recalled how his father used to be.

'Time we got on with finding this invention,' he thought grimly. 'Otherwise the Da's going to vanish into the bottle for good before we can haul him out.'

He and Nora and Sean took their turn at the oars. And at steering by the compass. Keeping their course as near to due east as they could.

And over the next few hours, as they rowed and drifted by turns across the quiet, sunny water, Sean, sometimes in answer to questions, at other times just when he felt like talking, told them more about himself.

# Chapter Thirty Three

He had known The Snapper, he said, for a long time. But it was only when his Mum and Dad were killed in the car crash, just over a year ago, that he had begun to realise that he could talk to The Snapper, and that The Snapper would talk back.

'I expect you know I've been living with my uncle Andy – my Da's younger brother,' Sean said. 'He's not a bad guy, but he's never there. He works long hours. Brings stuff home with him. And he doesn't know how to talk to me. Or me to him, either.

'It's been weird. My life changed so completely. From having Ma and Da, and lots of mates at school, suddenly I was on my own. There just seemed to be nobody.

'Uncle Andy lives in Dublin, right, and before I came here I lived down the country. So it was a big turn around every way. New school and all.

'My Ma had this old statue. Maybe it was a saint. But I used to talk to it, at night. It sort of seemed to bring her back. So about a year ago, it was weird, I felt he was talking back to me. I didn't tell anyone, right? They'd have thought I was wired up.

'Then one day, when I was lying about in the garden – it was a nice sunny day – this guy popped up out of nowhere.

'I wasn't too sure about him at first, right, but after he'd talked for a few minutes, I sort of knew he was all right. I could trust him, okay?

'So he told me he was called The Snapper, and said didn't I recognise him?

'And I suddenly knew that he was my statue – sort of come to life.

"You've been wanting something, Sean,' he said. 'Maybe I can help.'

' I didn't see how, but I'm all, like, 'I only wish you could.'

"So what do you mainly want?' he asked.

'So I'm, like, 'What about this knife thing? I don't know – did it have something to do with the car crash? Can I find out about it?'

And The Snapper said, 'You can if you really want to. But it won't change anything. I'm not into revenge, boy, and you needn't be either.'

'But it was just that I wanted to know, okay?'

'And I asked him if he could do something about getting me some friends, right? And he said he thought that was a much better idea. But he would see if he could do both.'

None of this came out at the same time. There were bits and pieces. Sean was finding it hard to talk freely about himself.

'But, Sean, I would have thought you could have had anyone you wanted as friends,' Nora said in amazement.

She thought, 'Isn't it weird how different people are, inside, from what they seem like, when you don't really know them?'

'Yeah?' Sean said. 'Well, anyway. The Snapper said he would take me back in time, to a place where I could get to know you lads, and maybe even help you a bit. He said it would do you no harm to manage mostly on your own, but a bit of help from me when it was needed would be good, too. And I would find out whatever I wanted to know about my knife. Next thing I found myself living in Cuchulain's time, and he seemed to think I was his best mate. It was ace!

'Then, after a while, you two turned up. That was really cool.

'I don't know why Cuchulain didn't catch on that I wasn't really Laeg. The real Laeg was on a trip somewhere else in time, I think. Snapper said he was okay – having a ball. And I think Snapper made Cuchulain think I looked like his mate.

'And the same sort of thing, the other times. There was always someone whose place I could take.

'So it was like – wow! But then when we got back home, and I met up with you, you didn't seem to recognise me. It threw me a bit.

'But it's better now, isn't it? We'll be able to hang out together when we get home?'

'Yeah, sweet!' agreed Jik

Nora grinned. 'You won't be able to get rid of us, Sean O'Reilly!' she predicted.

'Dead on,' was all Sean said, but they could see how pleased he was.

# Chapter 33

'Well,' said Jik eventually, 'you've found out some about your knife, man. And we've got to know each other. So I guess it's worked out for you. But Nora and I came on these trips for a good reason, and so far we've got nowhere.'

'Tell me about it,' Sean said. 'I know you said some stuff about an invention when we were with Cuchulain on the *White Lady*. But it seemed a bit mixed up, to tell you the truth. And when I asked Snapper, he said he would leave it to you to explain. Just like I had to explain to you.'

Jik and Nora, taking it in turn to speak, poured out their story. Talking to Sean, they were able to say much more about why they needed to do something about their father, than they had been able to do before, to adults like Grania.

'So you need to get back to Faraday's time?' Sean said at last, when he could understand. 'Easy-peasy. Just ask to go to the mid nineteenth century, or thereabouts.'

'Wow! You knew all along!' Jik said. 'If we'd had the sense to ask you before, we could have saved ourselves a lot of trouble!'

'But it's been great, hasn't it?' Nora said. 'I wouldn't have missed any of it.'

They had been so busy listening to Sean, and talking, that they had failed to notice what was happening to the galley.

'Hey!' Sean said suddenly. 'That looks to me like land, over there!'

It looked like an island. Small, but growing nearer every moment.

'Let's row faster!' suggested Jik. 'We must be nearly there.'

They pulled determinedly on the oars. Time passed. They could see the land clearly now, but it was still some distance away. They took turns at rowing, pushing on as fast as they could.

It was Sean's turn to steer.

'Look out!' he shouted suddenly. 'Rocks to port! Pull to starboard, Jik!'

Nora back paddled furiously, while Jik put his back into pulling to starboard.

'Wow!' said Sean. 'Just missed them. Keep to starboard, guys.'

'Nearly there,' he said a moment later.

'And then we'll be disappearing off home,' Nora said. 'Are you sure you'll be okay, Sean?'

'Definitely,' Sean grinned. 'Look, be sure to call at my uncle's! I'll see you there!'

'And will you meet up with us to go on *Lady Molly*?'

'No! I'll stick to my own arrangement with The Snapper!'

Then they felt the prow of the galley slipping up the yellow sand, and a moment later, the darkness. And waking up on the deck of the *Lady Molly*.

# Chapter Thirty Four

The next day the rain poured down and the wind blew a gale. It was no day for going out on *Lady Molly.*

Nora moped miserably around the house. She decided that she should write up her diary. There was lots to catch up on. She went up to her room looking for privacy. No way would she let Jik see her writing – he might try to find out what she was saying. Putting her hand confidently into the inside pocket of her jacket which was hanging on the hook of her bedroom door, she froze with horror. The diary wasn't there.

Then it was a matter of searching in every possible place, until nearly an hour later Nora realised that she was getting nowhere. The diary had gone, where she had no clue.

For a while she sat with her head in her hands, trying to hold back the tears. Where could it be? She knew she'd had it with her at the Internet Café. Had she dropped it there? Or if not, then in which of the many places where she'd been since?

There was no point in going on worrying. Nora tried to stop.

Presently she had a bright idea. It almost cheered her up. She ran downstairs to find Jik.

'Let's ring Sean,' she suggested. 'We didn't get his mobile number, stupid us, but what about trying for the landline?'

Jik, also feeling a bit down, perked up immediately.

'Cool!' he said. 'Go for it!'

The number was in the phone book, where they had found it before, under Andrew O'Reilly, at the uncle's address. Nora put it into her mobile and then rang it.

A moment later, there was Sean's voice saying, 'Hello?'

'Hi, Sean! It's me – Nora. And Jik. How ya doin'?'

'Ace,' said Sean's voice, sounding very cheerful. 'Are you going on the boat today?'

'Weather's too bad,' said Jik, who had grabbed Nora's phone from her as soon as he was sure that it was Sean himself on the other end. 'Maybe tomorrow.'

'Would you like to come over?'

'Yeah, great. See you soon, then.'

To Nora's annoyance, Jik switched off. There were lots of things she would have liked to say to Sean.

Boys! thought Nora. They've no idea!

Dragging on their jackets, they rushed for the bus.

It was a good day – every way except the weather.

Sean had a computer, and a snooker table. The fridge was full of exciting food. Sean seemed to be allowed to take what he wanted.

The hours flew by. It was no time at all till Jik and Nora decided, reluctantly, that they had better go home. Sean walked to the bus stop with them.

It was as they came round the first corner, that they walked straight into Marty Flanagan.

Marty Flanagan had picked on Jik and bullied him since Jik started at St Mary and St Joseph's.

Jik could joke about Marty Flanagan when he wasn't there, but meeting him face to face like this was a different matter.

He was glad Sean was with him. Nora wouldn't be much help, of course.

'Well, look who's here!' said Marty Flanagan in his most sneery voice. 'Supermouse himself!'

The nickname dated from the time when Jik had tried to rescue a smaller boy from Marty's bullying, and had ended up badly beaten up himself. That had been the start of Marty's regular attacks on him.

'Clear off, Flanagan!' said Sean briefly. 'Remember, none of your mates are with you tonight.'

Sean was at least as big as Marty. Nora hoped Marty would just go away.

'Clear off? Why should I?' Marty Flanagan blustered. 'What makes you think none of my mates are with me? There's at least one of them here, isn't that right, Cathga?'

Round the corner, strolling at his ease, came the Druid priest, whose name they had learnt on Grania's ship the *Seabird.* Cathga.

Nora knew that her face must have gone white.

How had he managed to track them down, to find out which time they came from, and where they lived?

'How did you find us?' she heard herself gasping out.

# Chapter 34

'So easily, my dear,' said Cathga. He held out a small blue-backed object which Nora recognised with horror.

Her diary!

Even at that moment, her skin crawled at the idea of anyone else, especially Sean, reading what she had written.

'One of you dropped this on the *Seabird*. You, was it, my dear? Yes, I thought it must be the little lady. It doesn't read like a man's production. So convenient, not only the address on the front page, but the date, even the year!' He smiled in a thoroughly nasty way. 'And the first person I met was Marty, here. And guess what? He was looking for you, too. Oh, Marty's been very helpful!'

Nora, her face now scarlet, tried to snatch the diary from Cathga's hands, but he held it above her reach, apparently enjoying her distress.

'Enough of the chit-chat!' interrupted Marty Flanagan. He made a quick lunge at Jik, and punched him in the eye before Jik had time to dodge. Sean, reacting straightaway, leapt in turn onto Flanagan's shoulders, and bore him down. The three boys rolled on the ground, kicking, punching and struggling.

Cathga strode forward. Putting out his considerable strength, he took Jik by the scruff of the neck in one hand and Sean in the other, and pulled them to their feet.

Marty Flanagan, released, shuffled upright, grinning unpleasantly.

'Stop!' commanded Cathga sternly.

He stood, holding the two boys so that their feet dangled helplessly above ground level.

'You have been guilty of blasphemy,' he said. He was looking at Sean. There was something in his eyes that turned Nora's blood to ice. 'You, and your father before you. Your father has paid the price. Now it is your turn. Only one thing will satisfy the spirits. Your throat must be slit with the sacred dagger you stole. Give me the knife of Bantha. I will carry out the requirements of the spirits now.'

Nora, alternately weeping and shouting with anger, tried to pull Cathga's grip loose from Sean, but with no result. The big man was even stronger than he seemed. He had no real need of Marty Flanagan's support, and Flanagan was contenting himself with kicking the two helpless boys as hard as he could manage.

It was when one of his kicks had gone slightly astray, and landed instead on Cathga's thigh, that the Druid priest turned round, his attention momentarily diverted from his prisoners, and said sternly to Marty Flanagan, 'Stop that!'

There was a tinkle as Sean's dagger, released from its home in his belt by Nora's tugs, fell at their feet. Before anyone else had noticed it, or realised what it was, Nora had pounced.

The dagger in one hand, she raced off down the avenue, heading for the main road, near, very near, but seeming so very far away, around the next corner.

Straight as a bird she flew, her feet barely touching the ground. No time now for tears or complaints. She must keep the dagger away from Cathga, that was all she knew.

She had only a moment's start before realisation struck, and feet began thundering after her.

Sobbing for breath, she rounded the corner, and ran straight into a big man carrying a briefcase, who grabbed her, laughing, and said, 'Whoa, whoa, what's this?'

'Oh, please!' Nora sobbed out, 'please don't let him! He's going to kill Sean!'

'Not if I know it!' exclaimed a friendly voice. 'Especially if you mean *my* Sean!'

It was Sean's Uncle Andy.

The big man strode forward towards the source of the trouble.

Before he could reach the druid, Cathga silently melted away. No one saw where he went.

So, too, a moment later, did Marty Flanagan, not so silently, pounding at top speed for the nearest bus stop on the main road.

# Chapter Thirty Five

A little blue book lay on the ground where the druid had been standing.

With a cry of thankfulness, Nora ran, lifted it, and thrust it deep in her pocket. Her diary.

Never again would she take it anywhere with her. It would remain at home, safely under lock and key. Never again would she run the risk that Sean might read its contents!

Perhaps, sometime soon, it might be the right time to let him guess a bit of what she felt. But that would be a very different thing!

Explanations were not easy. But eventually Uncle Andy understood that the school bully, together with an even more vicious adult, had been threatening them. He didn't take the actual threats seriously. But it was bad enough that they had been made. He would, he said, report it to the Garda as well as the school's head teacher.

While not seeing quite what good either action would do, they were happy enough, just now, to see the back of both Cathga and Flanagan. Hopefully Cathga had gone back to his own time. He had certainly vanished very abruptly, between one eye blink and another.

Sitting on the bus, later, Jik and Nora agreed that, somehow, they felt as if they had known Sean for years.

'He's a cool guy,' Jik said. It was his highest form of praise. 'And we get on with him just as well in ordinary life as when we're some time else.'

'Yeah,' agreed Nora. She said little about it. But inside she felt a bubbling excitement, as if all her dreams were coming true.

To their surprise, Colm was up and dressed, and was actually cooking them a meal.

They walked into the kitchen, drawn by the smell of fried mushrooms and bacon, and he greeted them, 'Hi, guys. Wondered where you were. Food'll soon be ready.'

'We were over at a mate's house,' Nora told him, although he hadn't asked.

When they were sitting round the table, Colm said, 'Sorry I haven't been around much these hols, lads.'

'Oh, that's okay, Da' said Jik. 'We've been having a good time on our own.'

Colm looked a bit disappointed.

'Well, we'll have to try to get together a bit more,' he said eventually. 'Go out on *Lady Molly*, maybe?'

Nora felt her face go red. She rushed hurriedly into speech.

'That would be great, Daddy. Sometime next week, perhaps?'

'Why leave it till then?' Colm asked. 'Let's plan it for the next good day, okay?'

Jik and Nora looked at each other in horror.

'Em – yeah, cool, Da,' Jik managed at last.

'I have to go out tonight,' Colm went on.

'So what's new?' thought Jik and Nora in silent chorus.

'But tomorrow, if it keeps clear, we'll get up in good time and go down to Howth, right?'

'Great, Daddy,' agreed Nora, trying not to sound as upset as she felt.

'What's up, lads?' asked Colm anxiously. 'I thought you'd be chuffed.'

'Oh, we are, Da,' Jik said. 'Just hoping it won't pour, like today.'

'Fair enough,' agreed Colm. 'That would be a bummer. But let's cheer up and hope for the best. Now, who's going to help me with these dishes? And then maybe we'd have time for that game of *Cluedo* that got interrupted the other night?'

The *Cluedo* was good.

Then Colm went out. 'As per usual,' thought Nora.

'I bet you he wants to take that Bridie Gallagher out with us on *Lady Molly*,' said Nora gloomily, when he had gone. 'That's why he's thought of it all of a sudden.'

'Could be,' agreed Jik. 'Well, so what? She's okay.'

Nora glared at him and Jik tactfully said no more.

'I tell you what,' Nora went on. 'We'd better get up and slip away down to the marina before the Da wakes up. Otherwise it'll be all messed up.'

'Right,' agreed Jik. 'No way the Da will be up early, anyway. You know what he's like. We could be there and back before he stirs, if we don't leave it too late ourselves.'

# Chapter 35

'Let's set the alarm, as if we were getting up for school,' Nora suggested.

It seemed like a good idea.

'And maybe we should go to bed a bit earlier than usual?'

Jik was less keen on this idea, but at last agreed.

'Though, mind you,' he said, 'if the Da's in anything like his usual state when he comes in, he'll be waking us both up with his noise at about two or three in the morning.'

But that evening Colm came home much earlier than usual. And far from waking them up, he crept so quietly up the stairs that Nora, reading herself to sleep, heard him only just in time to turn the light out and close her eyes before he opened her door softly and looked in at her.

'Asleep, pet?' she heard him murmur. 'Good girl.'

As she drifted off to sleep, Nora wondered why the Da was behaving so much better.

# Chapter Thirty Six

The alarm went off as planned.

Nora, struggling grumpily out of bed, went to shake Jik awake.

Ignoring his grumbles and dodging his flailing arm, she succeeded at last in bringing him back to life sufficiently to understand what was happening.

They slipped quietly downstairs and made some breakfast.

Then, bright and early, they left the house and headed for the marina.

Colm had also set his alarm.

He found it very hard to get up when the alarm went off. But he had promised the kids.

It looked like just the best sort of day for the boat. And he had promised Bridie to pick her up. She was taking the day off specially. Groaning, he forced himself out of bed.

Half an hour later, washed and dressed, he made his way downstairs.

No sign of the kids. Maybe they were still sleeping.

He went back upstairs. 'Rise and shine –' he began, putting his head round Jik's doorway. But there was no one there.

He went back down to the kitchen. Clearly they had been having breakfast. Colm turned on the kettle again, and wandered out into the garden.

No sign of them. It was pretty sickening, when he had got up on purpose.

Then, being basically a fair natured person, Colm reflected ruefully that they had every reason to expect that he wouldn't be up for some hours yet. Probably they had gone off somewhere not too far away, and would be back shortly.

He turned off the kettle, and then rang Bridie.

'The kids have disappeared – I expect they'll turn up soon. How about some brunch in the meantime?'

They met up at their local pub, the *Green Kitchen*, and ordered some food.

The ambience was old Irish. Whitewashed walls, dark beams, a turf fire and artefacts like a spinning wheel and a blackened cooking pot placed carefully about.

But the food was good.

'There's Danny Griffiths,' said Colm, when they had almost finished their soup and sandwiches. 'Haven't seen him for a while. Hi, Danny!'

'Colm, me old mate! Good to see you!'

The tall, sunburnt, man with the expansive air pulled out a chair, sat down beside them and began catching up on the gossip.

'So, Colm,' he said eventually, 'the kids were telling me you've been out on the *Lady Molly* again? It's been a while since you had her out.'

'The kids?' asked Colm sharply.

'Yep, young Jik and Nora. I ran into them the other day at the marina, heading for the boat. They told me you were picking up some stuff, and would be along shortly.'

Colm's face hardened. He sprang to his feet abruptly.

'Sorry, Danny. Got to go. Remembered something.'

He seized Bridie by the arm, paid at the bar, and hustled her out of the pub and across the car park in the bright summer sunshine.

'Let's get back home and check if the kids are there, love,' he said. 'And I'll look and see if the boat keys are where I left them, too!'

'But, Colm, you don't think –?'

'I don't know. But if they've been taking the boat out by themselves –! It's not safe, Bridie!'

A very few minutes were enough to show Colm that both his children and his boat keys were missing.

'I know this is my own fault, Bridie,' he said grimly. 'You were right to tell me I've been neglecting them. But if I find they've been going out on the boat by themselves –! I'll kill the pair of them!'

There was no time to lose. Moments later they were driving furiously towards Howth. They missed the *Lady Molly* by only a few minutes.

Colm looked wildly round.

There she was, bobbing along, heading out of the marina. Not too far away. But much too far to reach.

# Chapter 36

'Pat!' he shouted to a nearby friend. 'Any chance I can borrow your dinghy? I gotta go after my boat!'

'Sure you can, mate,' said the easy going Pat, staring at him. 'Go on ahead, then.'

Bundling Bridie first into the little dinghy, Colm jumped in and fired up the outboard motor. Pat obligingly cast off the mooring rope.

Dodging in and out of the other vessels, Colm followed the *Lady Molly* out of the marina and into the open sea.

'When we catch her, I'll haul alongside and hold the dinghy steady while you scramble up, Bridie,' Colm said. 'Do you think you can manage?'

Bridie, who wasn't a bit sure, nevertheless nodded.

'Right, so then I'll fasten on the dinghy and be straight up after you.'

In a very short space of time, they were bumping against the *Lady Molly's* stern.

No one on board noticed them at first. Both Jik and Nora were focussed on The Snapper, listening carefully as he gave them a few words of warning.

'I've been giving you a free rein, lads. I reckon you've learned plenty on these trips. About yourselves, right? Even if you haven't learnt much about old Peter's invention! But we can't go on like this, getting nowhere, forever. You've made a good choice this time. Thought it out, for a change. Stopped treating it like a game. Starting to grow up a bit, maybe? So I don't want you messing this up like you did last time. Right, maties?'

'Right, Snapper,' they both said.

'Okay, then. Hold tight,' Snapper said, just as Bridie half clambered, half fell, over the rail of the boat. A moment later, Colm's head appeared, coming after her.

It was already growing dark, and the boat was beginning its alarming pitching motion. Jik and Nora, with their backs to the stern rail, were too busy clinging on to the bench to notice the new arrivals.

But The Snapper, looking over their shoulders towards the stern of the boat, saw what was happening.

Leaping forward, he was just in time to seize Colm and drag him the rest of the way on board, before it was too late.

'Talk about a daft thing to do!' he growled. He went on muttering furiously to himself. 'Climbing on board when you didn't know what villains might have taken the boat! You were always half daft, Colm Lavery! You nearly got caught in the hole between the time zones! Well, it's too late to stop it now! You'll just have to go along, too – you and your girlfriend! The kids will explain when you get there.'

Then there was no time to say any more.

There was nothing but the darkness and the wild pitching, rough as the roughest storm.

# Chapter Thirty Seven

To Colm, it seemed to go on forever.

Then the darkness began to clear.

The rain was lashing down. Jik and Nora huddled together under the nearest sail. The rain made it hard to see, but it seemed to be still daylight. The boat they were on, whatever it was, had settled down and was pitching much less furiously

Colm and Bridie rushed towards them.

'Jik!' roared Colm at the top of his voice.

Jik and Nora looked round.

'Da!'

They could hardly believe that Colm and Bridie were really there.

'What in the name of all the saints are you kids up to?' Colm yelled. 'I thought you promised me you wouldn't try to take the boat out by yourselves?'

His face was black with rage. Mixed with the anger, and the main cause of it, was an overwhelming fear at the risk they had been taking.

'Before you say anything more, Da,' Jik said quickly, 'we're sorry to have taken *Lady Molly* out without your permission. But we didn't break our promise to you and take her out by ourselves. The Snapper was with us every time. He said you knew him, and it would be okay.'

'The Snapper?' asked Colm in amazement.

'Yeah, you know,' said Nora, 'St Stormy Weather, the seamen's saint, you used to call him? The statue in the church?'

'He's been taking us back into the past, to find out about great Granda Peter's invention, so we can put in a claim to it,' Jik explained.

Colm stared at them, for a moment speechless. All the anger seemed to have been knocked out of him by shock, as he gradually realised what was happening.

'But why –? What on earth for –?' was all he could manage.

'So that you could feel you had something to be proud of. We hoped it would give you back some self-respect. Stop you drinking so much! Things have been so awful, lately!' Nora rushed into speech without much forethought.

Then she saw Colm's face. He had turned first red, then white. It occurred to both Jik and Nora that perhaps they had been a bit too forthright.

Colm seemed unable to speak. It was Bridie who intervened.

'And have you found it yet, lads?' she asked. Her voice showed nothing but ordinary curiosity and interest.

'Not so far,' stammered Jik, thankful for the chance to move the conversation on. He could not bear to see his father so stricken.

'I'm so sorry, Daddy,' wailed Nora. 'I didn't mean –'

'Yes, you did, sweetheart.' Colm spoke quite softly. 'And you were quite right. I've been in a bad way since your mum died. I've been drinking and drinking, trying to cure the pain that way. It hasn't worked. But now I'm trying to stop. I really am. Bridie here has been a great help. I don't know that finding old Peter's invention and claiming it will make all that difference.'

'Oh.'

His children looked at him.

'We were trying to help, Da,' Jik said at last.

'I see that, kids,' Colm said.

'Hey! What are you people doing above deck?'

A loud, harsh voice made them jump. They turned round.

A tall man, dressed like Russell Crowe in *Master and Commander*, in a smart frock coat fastened with shiny brass buttons, and white breeches, with a pale, bony face, was striding across the deck towards them. He wore high leather boots, and an air of authority mixed with anger.

'Don't you know these are the crews' quarters? All passengers below decks!'

He began to push them towards the nearby companionway.

'No disobedience aboard the *Betsy Jane*! My officers and I see to it that orders are obeyed at all times. We don't want passengers getting in the way and causing trouble.'

As he spoke, he herded them briskly down the ladder to a dark, stuffy compartment crowded with people.

'And be sure you stay there!' he finished.

It seemed best to obey, at first. At least until they found out where they were and what was happening.

'Jik?' Colm asked. He had taken in that they were in another time zone. 'You and Nora seem to have some experience of this stuff. What is likely to happen next?'

'And do you know where we are?' put in Bridie.

'Well,' said Jik cautiously, 'we asked to come to the mid nineteenth century. But I was hoping to be on the *Nancy Belle*. I haven't a clue why we've ended up on this *Betsy Jane* ship, instead.'

They were beginning to see a little better, now, as their eyes grew accustomed to the darkness.

'They're packed in like sardines,' Nora thought, looking at the people crammed into all the available space. They were sitting or lying on all sides, on bunks and in hammocks. Many of them were groaning. Their faces were thin and pale. There were coughs coming from all directions. Were they seasick? Or was there something more serious wrong with some of them? It was hard to tell.

Nearest to her was a pale, thin woman, cuddling a little boy of about three. She was trying to keep him warm, wrapping him in a shawl. The shawl was very ragged, and she had probably, Nora thought, taken it from round her own shoulders to wrap the child. Nora knelt down beside her, dragging off her jacket.

'Here, put this round your little boy!' she said impulsively. 'You need the shawl for yourself.'

The woman smiled weakly and thanked her.

'The sailor said he would try to get some blankets for us.'

'Who was that?'

'A young lad – fair hair. Name of Ryan. He went away a while ago to look.'

Nora felt her heart thumping with excitement.

Could it be? Was it? She felt sure it must be Sean.

Colm was kneeling beside a thin bearded man who was stretched out on the bare boards beneath a high porthole.

'Steven Murphy,' the man was saying in answer to Colm's questions. 'From near Galway. Me and my family walked thirty miles to get to this boat. We planned to set sail for the New World. Get away from the hunger and the need all round us at home. I hear there's a chance in other countries for any man who's prepared to work. And I'm that, believe me.'

Colm asked. 'Are you ill?'

'Not exactly, I think,' said Steven Murphy. 'It's just the walking on top of the hunger. A decent meal would maybe sort me out.'

'We'll see what we can do,' said Colm.

He stood up.

'Bridie. Kids,' he said. 'I've a pretty good idea now where we've got to. This must be the time of the Potato Famine. And I'm sorry to have to tell you –'

He paused and looked at them.

'I think we're on one of the famine ships, headed for America.'

# Chapter Thirty Eight

They gazed at him open mouthed.

'These poor people,' said Bridie at last. 'They've been through so much. And now this horrific journey on top of everything.'

The sound of feet clattered down the companionway.

'Hi,' said a familiar voice. 'Can you grab some of these blankets?'

'Sean!' cried Nora joyfully.

'Ryan,' said the young sailor. But he winked at Nora and Jik as he said it.

They helped him to distribute the blankets to the most needy people.

Colm spoke firmly to the person he thought of as Ryan.

'Who's in charge here? Most of these people need food more than anything else.'

'Captain Hamilton, sir,' replied Ryan promptly.

'Then take me to him at once.'

Ryan turned to lead Colm up the ladder.

They found the captain sprawling at ease in his comfortable cabin in the stern of the *Betsy Jane*. It was the same tall, bony faced man who had chased them down below decks not long ago, but he failed to recognise Colm. Beside him, his back turned to Colm and Ryan, was his mate, bending over, busily engaged in drawing lines on a chart. Neither Colm nor Ryan could see his face.

Colm addressed the captain sharply.

'You, sir! You are the captain of this ship?'

'I am, sir,' replied Captain Hamilton. He raised his eyebrows haughtily. 'And who may you be?'

'My name is Lavery, Captain. And may I inform you that my purpose on board this ship is specifically to check that you, and others in similar ships, are supplying the passengers with sufficient food and water for this voyage.' Colm glared at Hamilton.

'Money has been contributed for this purpose, sir. If I report back that it has not been used correctly, but has gone into the pocket of the captain, then that captain will be severely dealt with. He will be brought to justice, sir!'

Captain Hamilton's jaw fell.

He began to fall over himself to pacify this angry man who he thought must be a government representative.

'I assure you, sir, the passengers on my ship are extremely well fed! In fact, a meal is due now, so you can see for yourself!'

He rang a hand bell on the table beside his comfortable chair.

A sailor appeared quickly.

'Simpson, time to feed the passengers. See that there's plenty for all. Bread and meat and fruit, as much as they need.'

Simpson didn't seem to be the brightest. He gaped at the captain, and began to question him.

'One slice of bread, we've been giving them, captain. Do you mean you want me to change the rations?'

'Nonsense, man!' roared the captain. 'They should be getting the same as the crew, don't you understand that?'

He hustled the man out of the cabin, and turned ingratiatingly back to Colm.

'Go with him and see for yourself, sir,' he suggested. 'They get only the best, just the same as my men.'

'Come with me, Ryan,' Colm said to Sean, who had been listening to him in admiration. With a final glare at the captain, he followed the sailor.

In the crowded cabin below decks, the other three were doing their best to help the rest of the passengers. One woman in particular worried Nora.

She seemed even thinner than most of them, but far from being pale, her face was hot and flushed, and she was tossing and turning about on the narrow bunk until Nora was afraid she would fall out.

Nora knelt beside her, trying to hold the woman securely, unsure what else she should do. Bridie's voice spoke in her ear.

'I'm afraid she has a bad fever. Perhaps she would drink some water. I think there's some in the barrel over there.'

Thankful to have something to do, Nora sprang up.

'I'll get some for her,' she promised.

There was a metal cup beside the barrel. Nora gave it a quick rinse and filled it two thirds full.

When she came back, Bridie was rootling in her shoulder bag.

## Chapter 20

'I know I have some paracetamol here somewhere,' she said. 'Ah – got it.'

'These tablets dissolve in water, thank goodness,' she went on. 'I don't know if she could swallow them, otherwise.'

Taking the cup from Nora, she dropped two tablets into the water, and waited for a minute until they were dissolved. Then, carefully holding the cup to the woman's lips, she helped her to drink it down.

In a remarkably short time, the woman was lying peacefully, drifting off into sleep. Her face no longer seemed hot and flushed.

Nora looked on in amazement. Bridie, seeing her expression, laughed.

'The miracle drug, they called it, when Fleming first invented aspirin. Paracetamol is much the same, but better for you. It wasn't invented when these poor people were around, I'm afraid. It's supposed to have been the biggest breakthrough in modern medicine. Probably saved more lives than anything since. And we take it for granted!'

'Oh, Bridie, thank you!' Nora said impulsively. 'You're the best!'

'Don't thank me. I've done nothing. But let's see if we can help anyone else.'

'Right.'

Jik was still engaged in carrying blankets to and fro. When Colm arrived back with Ryan and the sailors who were bringing the food, he found all three of them working busily.

Nora and Bridie had given paracetamol to several other feverish people, and the moaning, which had distressed them all when they first came into the passengers' quarters, had to a great extent died away.

Colm and Ryan, with the grudging help of the sailors, made sure that everyone had a good meal.

'I only wish we could do this for every ship that carried famine victims to America,' Colm said.

'You can't change history,' Bridie said. 'All you can do is help the people you actually meet up with. Be glad that at least one ship load will get to America without most of the passengers dying on the way.'

'Yes,' agreed Colm.

'They need some fresh air, too,' Bridie said briskly. 'Is the rain over?'

'Yeah.'

'Then let's get the ones who are fit enough up onto the deck, when they've finished eating.'

So presently they were helping most of the passengers to climb the companionway, and get the first draft of fresh air they had had since the start of the voyage.

They were leaning against the railing on the port side, when two tough looking sailors came over to them. One of them addressed Colm in a nasty voice.

'What's going on here?'

Then he stopped abruptly.

'It's that government inspector fella!' he muttered to his companion. 'I'm outa here!'

He scuttled off without another word.

# Chapter Thirty Nine

The companion, however, remained behind. He was a much pleasanter looking man, big and tough, certainly, but with a face creased with laugh lines and a humorous expression in his dark eyes.

'Don't I know you from somewhere, sir?' he asked.

'I don't think so. My name's Lavery. Colm Lavery.'

'That's it!' exclaimed the man. 'I'm thinking of Peter Lavery, a good friend of mine. You're his spit an' image. Not just the red hair – it's in the shape of the face, and all. We sailed together on the *Nancy Belle*. Before she sank, that was. Then I got a berth on the *Betsy Jane*. Not such pleasant officers, and a lower rank for me, but you have to take what you can get, when you've let your ship sink.'

'You knew old Peter!' Colm exclaimed.

'Not so old as all that!' the sailor laughed. 'Within a year of my own age, and yours, too, I'd guess!'

Colm thought quickly. 'Right! He's a relation of mine. I'd be interested to know what you can tell me about him.'

The sailor relaxed against the rail, and took out a smelly old pipe. He filled it, and began to puff at it as he spoke.

'Peter and I have the same name. Peter O'Donnell, that's me. So we first struck up a friendship on that basis. We found we got on well. He was captain of the *Nancy Belle* and I was mate. But he never pulled rank on me.

'He was a man with a great interest in science. He tried to talk to me about it at first, but he soon saw that it meant nothing to me, and he stopped then.

'But he spent most of his free time fiddling away with wires and stuff he had rigged up in his cabin. Doing experiments, he said.

'Then one day he told me he had worked out something important. He wasn't ready to tell the world just yet, but sailors would bless him for it when it came into use. That same night came the storm that did for the *Nancy Belle*.

'We were all milling around in the dark with the waves lashing at us, doing our best to keep her afloat. We were hoping the old ship would survive it yet. Then the mast was struck by lightening.

'That was the end. Peter Lavery was struck on the head by a falling spar, but he kept on his feet and worked away, cutting loose the rigging to clear the decks.

'It was too late, though. Nothing to be done.

'Not many minutes later, Captain Lavery was shouting 'Abandon ship!'

'We got most of the crew into the lifeboat, but there was no room for us. Peter and I went overboard together, the last to go. He was holding a packet in one hand, wrapped up careful in oilcloth.

'He said to me, 'Pete, you've been a good mate to me. I don't think I can hold on much longer. I'm feeling pretty dizzy from that bang on the head.'

'We had both got hold of a spar, see, and were clinging on to that in the swelling seas, hoping and praying to survive till a rescue ship got to us.'

'Pete,' he said, 'I want you to take this package. It's all the notes on my experiments, and the results. You're a bigger, stronger man than me. I reckon you're more likely to hold on. If you get safely home out of this, give it to Michael Faraday. Or better still, to my family first. Tell them to talk to Faraday about it.'

'Then he thrust the packet at me, and I took it.

'It seemed long enough before a rescue ship picked us up. Peter was in a bad way. They carried him off to hospital. I lost contact with him after that.

'But if you're his family, sir, it seems you should get the packet, for what it's worth.'

Colm found it difficult to speak.

Then, 'I'd be very grateful for it,' he said.

Jik and Nora held their breath. They could hardly believe that the end of their search had come so close.

'Then, if you'll wait here, I'll fetch it. I've kept it safe with my private belongings for the last six months. Tell me, did Peter survive?'

'Yes, he survived, all right,' Colm told him. He stopped himself in time from adding, 'and lived to a ripe old age.'

'Good.'

# Chapter 20

Peter O'Donnell disappeared in search of the package. No one spoke while they waited. Presently he returned, and thrust a bulky, salt stained bundle at Colm.

'Here you are, Colm. I hope it's of some value to you.'

Colm took the packet with trembling hands.

'It is.'

'It's a strange thing, to me, that you should be a government inspector, now,' said Peter O'Donnell. 'I would have put you down as a sailor, myself.'

Colm laughed. 'Oh, I'm not strictly speaking a government inspector. I gave the captain that impression just to see to it that he fed the passengers properly!'

'What!'

There was a roar of anger from behind him.

Unseen by anyone, Captain Hamilton and his mate had come up beside them. Near enough to hear Colm's last statement.

'You cheating ruffian! I couldn't make out how a government man got aboard without me knowing! So it was all a con! I'll have you all whipped and put in the brig for that!'

As he spoke, Jik and Nora saw the mate for the first time.

Cathga.

This was disaster.

Jik and Nora looked at each other. No way they would be escaping home for hours yet. The nearest land must be hundreds of miles away.

What were they to do?

Colm looked pale.

'Sorry, kids. Bridie,' he said briefly. 'My fault for opening my big mouth.'

Bridie squeezed his arm gently. 'Don't be daft.'

'I'll see them into the brig, Captain,' volunteered the mate. Cathga. 'Let them cool their heels there for a while. We can see to the whipping presently.' He hustled them together, gripping Ryan especially tightly.

The Captain grunted approval.

'I'll be on the bridge when you're ready, mate,' he said. Glaring at the prisoners over his shoulder, he strode off.

'Now,' said Cathga, 'the dagger, please.'

'Don't give it to him, Sean!' cried Nora sharply. 'You know what he wants it for!'

'Yes. But,' said Sean, 'maybe if I give it to him, he'll let the rest of you go!'

'No!' cried Nora.

Sean reluctantly pulled the dagger from his belt.

The Druid's eyes gleamed. His hands, releasing their grasp of Sean's arm, went out towards the dagger.

Just at that moment, whirling round away from the priest, Sean hurled the dagger towards the edge of the deck.

It should have gone overboard. It should have been lost forever in the depths of the mid Atlantic ocean.

Instead it stuck, quivering, in the wooden bulwark.

Jik gave a hoarse cry and rushed forward.

Cathga, at first thunderstruck, recovered his wits and was only seconds behind him.

Jik wrestled with the dagger, freed it with a mighty effort, and hurled it far into the ocean.

This time there was nothing to stop it.

With a despairing wail, Cathga leapt for the rails.

He gave one more unearthly cry, then plunged into the depths. His head vanished beneath the waves. There was nothing anyone could have done to stop him.

'Hold hands!' Sean shouted. 'Quick, before the Captain comes back!'

He grabbed Nora and Jik by one hand each. Responding instantly, Nora seized Bridie's hand. Even at that dreadful moment, she had a fleeting thought of amazement that she should be doing this. Bridie had been great with all those sick people, she thought. Nora had been wrong about her, not giving her a chance. If they got back safely things would be different, she resolved. She squeezed Bridie's hand, and smiled at her shyly.

Bridie smiled back.

At the same moment, Jik grabbed hold of his father's hand. Colm and Bridie were already clinging to each other.

'Snapper! It's time to go home, now!' called Sean. 'All of us, please! Not just me!'

# Chapter Forty

There was a sudden roaring, and the *Nancy Belle* lurched sharply and began to roll from side to side in a terrifying manner. They found themselves hurled across the deck in the familiar way.

'Hold on!' Sean tried to say, but his voice was carried away by the fierce winds.

Darkness fell.

It was impossible to move, to speak, to do anything except cling on tightly to each other.

Then suddenly it was light again. The huge surges stopped. They were no longer shaken from side to side.

'We're home!' gasped Nora.

They stood, still hand in hand, on the familiar deck of the *Lady Molly*.

'Thank you, Ryan!' Colm said after a breathless moment. 'I don't know what you did, but you certainly kept your head and did it!'

'My name's really Sean, Mr Lavery.'

'Call me Colm.'

'Sean's our best friend, Daddy,' explained Nora. 'He's come with us on our trips into the past and saved us lots of times. And now he's saved you and Bridie, too.'

'It wasn't me, Mr Lavery – Colm, I mean,' Sean said. 'It was this guy.'

They looked round.

There stood The Snapper beside them, his face creased in smiles.

'Congratulations!' he said, his blue eyes twinkling. 'You got rid of the druids' knife once for all! You can be sure it'll not rise again from the ocean depths until Judgement Day. And you found Peter Lavery's secret. So now, what are you going to do with it, Colm?'

Colm looked rather dazed. He couldn't really be talking to a statue, could he?

But after everything else that had happened? Perhaps he could?

He said, 'I'll start by taking it to a friend of mine, an expert in this sort of thing. I'll get his opinion on it first. Then I'll pull out all the stops to see Peter Lavery gets the acknowledgement for his pioneer work on radar that he deserves.'

'Good man!' said The Snapper. 'Well, young Jik? Well, Nora? Satisfied? Can I go back and report, 'Job done', eh?'

'I guess so,' Jik said hesitatingly.

'It wasn't just about that, Snapper,' Nora said.

'I know,' said Snapper. 'But that bit's not up to me.'

A moment later, with a last wink at Colm, he was gone.

Colm flushed.

'I know what else it was about,' he said. 'Finding the invention is great, but it wouldn't make that much difference to how I've been, guys. But I'll tell you what *is* making a difference. Knowing how hard you lads worked to get me sane again! And Bridie – you're the best! I swear to all of you, I won't waste what you've done. I'll make sure you see a difference in me from now on!'

'Oh, Daddy!'

Nora hugged him.

Colm put his arm round Jik and hugged him too.

'I don't know what all the fuss was about,' Sean said abruptly. 'What I've seen, your dad is really ace! You should have seen him dealing with that Captain Hamilton!'

'Hey, whoa, cool it!' protested Colm.

Bridie punched his arm playfully.'Wow, soon be putting you in for the 'Father of the Year', big man.'

She winked at Jik, Nora and Sean. They grinned happily back.

Colm laughed. 'Enough, already!' he said. 'Hey, I'm starving! Time we got this boat back to her mooring, and all go for a pizza together, right? Okay with you guys?'

It was okay.

# About the author

Gerry McCullough has been writing poems and stories since childhood. Brought up in north Belfast, she graduated in English and Philosophy from Queen's University, Belfast, then went on to gain an MA in English.

She lives just outside Belfast, in Northern Ireland, has four grown up children and is married to author, media producer and broadcaster, Raymond McCullough, with whom she co-edited the Irish magazine, *Bread*, (published by *Kingdom Come Trust*), from 1990-96. In 1995 they published a non-fiction book called, *Ireland – now the good news!*

Over the past few years Gerry has had more than fifty short stories published in UK, Irish and American magazines, anthologies and annuals – as well as broadcast on *BBC Radio Ulster* – plus poems and articles published in several Northern Ireland and UK magazines. She has also read from her novel, poems and short stories at many Irish literary events.

Gerry won the *Cúirt International Literary Award* for 2005 (Galway); was shortlisted for the 2008 *Brian Moore Award* (Belfast); shortlisted for the 2009 *Cúirt Award*; and commended in the 2009 *Seán O'Faolain Short Story Competition*, (Cork).

*Belfast Girls,* her first full-length Irish novel, was first published (by *Night Publishing*, UK) in November 2010. *Danger Danger* was published by *Precious Oil Publications* in October 2011; followed by *The Seanachie: Tales of Old Seamus* in January 2012 (a first collection of humorous Irish short stories, previously published in a weekly Irish magazine); and *Angel in Flight: an Angel Murphy thriller* in June 2012.

The *Cúirt Award* winning story, *Primroses*, and the *Seán O'Faolain* commended story, *Giving Up*, will be included in a new collection of twelve Irish short stories written by Gerry, to be published shortly. Also in the pipeline is *Not the End of the World* – a humorous, futuristic, adult fantasy novel.

More info at:

**gerrymccullough.com**
**gerrysbooks.blogspot.com**

Adult fiction by *Gerry McCullough*

# The Seanachie:
## *Tales of Old Seamus*

A humorous series of Irish stories, set in the fictional Donegal village of Ardnakil and featuring that lovable rogue, *'Old Seamus'* – the Séanachie.

All of these stories have previously been published in the popular Irish weekly magazine, *Ireland's Own*, based in Wexford, Ireland.

*"heart warming tales ... beautifully told with subtle Irish humour"*

**Babs Morton (author)**

*"an irresistible old rogue, but he's the kind people love to sit and listen to for hours on end whenever the opportunity presents itself"*

**G. Polley (author and blogger – Sapporo, Japan)**

*"This magnificent storyteller has done it again. Each individual story has it's own Gaelic charm"*

**Teresa Geering (author – UK)**

*"evocative characterisation brings these stories to life in a delightful, absorbing way"*

**Elinor Carlisle (author – Reading, UK)**

Adult fiction by **Gerry McCullough**

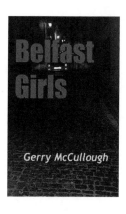

# Belfast Girls

The story of three girls – Sheila, Phil and Mary – growing up into the new emerging post-conflict Belfast of money, drugs, high fashion and crime; and of their lives and loves.

Sheila, a supermodel, is kidnapped. Phil is sent to prison. Mary, surviving a drug overdose, has a spiritual awakening.

It is also the story of the men who matter to them –

John Branagh, former candidate for the priesthood, a modern Darcy, someone to love or hate. Will he and Sheila ever get together? Davy Hagan, drug dealer, 'mad, bad and dangerous to know'. Is Phil also mad to have anything to do with him?

Although from different religious backgrounds, starting off as childhood friends, the girls manage to hold on to that friendship in spite of everything.

A book about contemporary Ireland and modern life. A book which both men and women can enjoy – thriller, romance, comedy, drama – and much more ….

*"fascinating ... original ... multilayered ... expertly travels from one genre to the next"*

**Kellie Chambers**, **Ulster Tatler** (Book of the Month)

*"romance at the core ... enriched with breathtaking action, mystery, suspense and some tear-jerking moments of tragedy.*

**Sheila M. Belshaw**, author

*"What starts out as a crime thriller quickly evolves into a literary festival beyond the boundary of genres"*

**PD Allen**, author

Adult fiction by **Gerry McCullough**

# Danger Danger

Two lives in parallel – twin sisters separated at birth, but their lives take strangely similar and dangerous roads until the final collision which hurls each of them to the edge of disaster.

Katie and her gambling boyfriend Dec find themselves threatened with peril from the people Dec has cheated.

Jo-Anne (Annie), through her boyfriend Steven, finds herself in the hands of much more dangerous crooks.

Can they survive and achieve safety and happiness?

Adult fiction by **Gerry McCullough**

# Angel in Flight:

## an Angel Murphy thriller

**Is it a bird? Is it a plane?
No, it's a low-flying Angel!**

**You've heard of Lara Croft.
You've heard of Modesty Blaise.
Well, here comes Angel Murphy!**

Angel, a *'feisty wee Belfast girl'* on holiday in Greece, sorts out a villain who wants to make millions for his pharmaceutical company by preventing the use of a newly discovered malaria vaccine.

Angel has a broken marriage behind her and is wary of men, but perhaps her meeting with Josh Smith, who tells her he's with Interpol, may change her mind?

Fun, action, thrills, romance in a beautiful setting – so much to enjoy!

*"evocative prose, realistic characterisation and brilliant dialogue make this a thriller which grips you from first page to last"*
**Elinor Carlisle** *(author, Berkshire, UK)*

*"A thriller that packs a real punch …
goes way beyond the surface thrills of boy meets girl."*
**Sooz Burke** *(author, Australia)*

*"something really different … the first of a new series featuring the spirited and energetic and very, very attractive heroine"*
**Sheila Mary Belshaw** (author, UK, Menorca & Cape Town)

*"a tough little devil and a charming Irish gal …
with a sassy brogue and kick-butt attitude"*
**Barbara Silkstone** (author, Florida, USA)

Non-fiction books from

# A Wee Taste a' Craic:

All the Irish craic from the popular **Celtic Roots Radio** shows, 2-25

## *Raymond McCullough*

*"I absolutely loved this!*
*I found it to be very informative about Irish life culture, language and traditions."*
**Elinor Carlisle** (author, **Reading, UK**)

*"a unique insight into the Northern Irish people*
*& their self deprecating sense of humour"*
**Strawberry (Northern Ireland)**

*"I loved your commentary and explanations of*
*N. Ireland's unmistakable wit and sense of humor.*
**Jerry McLean** (Irish musician, **Los Angeles, USA**)

*"My history is Irish so I love learning new things about the country!"*
**Sage Burnish (Athens, Georgia, USA)**

*Ireland* – now the <u>good</u> news!

**The best of *'Bread'* Vols. 1 & 2 –**

**personal testimonies and church/fellowship profiles from around Ireland**

Edited by: **Raymond & Gerry McCullough**

*"... fresh Bread – deals with the real issues facing the church in Ireland today"*
**Ken Newell** (minster of **Fitzroy Presbyterian Church, Belfast** )

Check out our website for more inspiring books from

## *Precious Oil Publications*

*http://www.preciousoil.com/publications*

13960270R00103

Printed in Great Britain
by Amazon.co.uk, Ltd.,
Marston Gate.